WONDERLESS

SHELBY RAEBECK

gatekeeper press™

Columbus, Ohio

WONDERLESS

for Talia and Sebastian

BOOK ONE

1

On one side of my room in Uncle Lanny's third floor apartment is the door, leading each morning out and down to school, and on the other side the window, my evening portal into the fire escapes circling the courtyard, stacked from the second story to the sixth.

My fourth floor buddy, Connie, has an older brother marine, captain of a mountaineering unit went to Afghanistan, who hooks us up with ropes, cables, pulleys, harnesses, three of us setting up a mad cool network of zip lines, cutting corners, crisscrossing open space, keeps us out later and later.

Isn't long before Lanny receives a letter from the District Office saying the tardies and missed detentions have exceeded the limit, and I've been assigned to meet with District Psychologist Bindermaus, his office at the end of my block, corner of 48th and 9th.

"Little Man," Dr. Bindermaus says from behind his desk, "all your important classes are in the morning."

"Day starts too early," I say. "And Astronomy isn't till period nine."

"Astronomy's an elective," he says.

"I've been electin to read science books since I was four," I say.

When a year earlier, my mom sent me off from the Bronx to Lanny's in Hell's Kitchen, she was sure to pack the science book series she'd been adding to over the years, every birthday and Christmas—*Primates, Geology of North America, Marine Life, Space and Time, Dark Energy.*

"I think you're headed down a slippery slope," Bindermaus says.

I shrug my shoulders.

"Easier to get back on track sooner than later," he says.

"Nah, if I'm off it, I'm off it," I say.

"I think you might be holding on to some grief."

"You talking about my mom giving me up?"

Dr. B sits there looking at me with his moon eyes.

Although Social Services had made the call, my mom and I agreed the move made sense, Uncle Lanny, like my dad, being an Iraqi war vet, only Lanny lost half a lung and collects disability.

"Gravity pulls bodies down to earth," I say, "but dark energy, which is 68 percent of everything, pulls them back out to space."

"It pulled you away from your mother?" he says.

"Didn't have to," I say. "She wasn't holding on."

Couple nights later, that April daylight-savings sun dropping past the roofline, Connie and I meet up in the scapes, slinging, clambering, affixing clamps and cable, installing new routes, angling down, one floor to the next, climb back up, settle on our haunches on the level two landing where we peep Dr. B's office, kids in there gathering for Thursday evening group.

Five boys of assorted shapes and shades settle into the sofa and chairs, arranged in a circle, all of em hang dog, Dr. B sitting with his back to the window, elbows on knees, leaning toward his wards, one of them, skinny white kid with blotchy skin and a buzzcut, gazing past him out the window, up toward where Connie and I sit, not seeing but sensing us.

The following Thursday, Connie and I are on the first landing bolt-clamping more cables when outside Dr. B's open window, a slim figure walks beneath us, jumps up and grabs the bottom rung, pulls himself up five more with only his arms, and joins us on the first landing.

"You a rangy dude," I say.

"I guess," kid with blotchy skin says.

Moved here from Iowa a year ago to live with his cousin, so we call him Seed, take him up the scape, then back down, staying off the newly strung cables till we can fit him with a harness, and the next Thursday, the three of us watch from the first landing as more of the groggy unborn, including two dudes got kicked off the high school basketball team, Moses the big man and Smiley the point guard, gather in Dr. B's office.

We collect tiny pebbles from the rooftop to rain down against Dr. B's window, and before long, Moses slips from the circle, raises the lower sash, squeezes his big frame out into the courtyard, locates the ladder, and ascends. Then Smiley, shorter, stockier, comes slithering out, Dr. B behind him absorbed in the circle.

Little later, a third guy, lighter-skinned, slips out and climbs up, telling us how he came from Tunisia, his dad having to sell his taxi so he could buy him a ticket to New York and put him on a plane with six hundred dollars. We call him Muzzy.

We knock on Connie's living room window, send the newbies in for gear, Connie's brother restocked, saying he'll cover these guys but from now on dudes are going to have to pony up.

Spring days growing longer, I sit above the courtyard on the roof edge of my building as the darkness begins to thicken, creating a film against the city light, each night a few more creatures emerging from windows, from the dark mouths of alleys, on Thursdays through Bindermaus's window, nylon harnesses rustling, carabiners clinking, figures gliding before me through dim shafts of light from shade-drawn windows.

Drizzly Saturday afternoon, few of us grab sodas at Pablo's on 48th, huddling beneath the awning out front, and it comes out that Smiley's sister, Tanika, and this sassy, round-faced chick from my Astronomy class, Sheila Camato, have been climbing in Bryant Park.

Courtyard maxed out anyway, once the rain stops and night comes, the six of us go check them out, entering off 6th Avenue, sitting on a bench, gazing up at the light gathering against the leafy ceiling.

After a few minutes, we walk further in, a few solitary figures slumped on benches along the path, hear a rustle above, then nothing.

Unable to see through the canopy of leaves, I lead the others up the nearest lamp post, balance on the post's glass dome and one-arm it through the leafy shield into the darkness, find a branch thick enough to hold.

Inside, our eyes adjust and we continue up a rope ladder rising through twisted branches to a small plank landing where we see a cable across an air hollow leading to more ladders, free hanging ropes, wood-plank landings, zip lines.

"What the fuck you doing, Smiley?" says a voice from above.

"Chillin," Smiley says.

"What about you, Little Man?" says a second voice, sounds like Sheila.

"Chillin with my boys," I answer.

"You all snoopin," first voice says.

"How many you got up here, Tanika?" Smiley asks.

"Too many now," Sheila says, and we hear a rustle of leaves and see a long body, must be Tanika, who's half a head taller than Smiley, fly off into space and disappear in the darkness. Then more rustling, and the three of us twist our necks to see Sheila ascending a higher ladder, stopping to take in the view, holding on with one hand, passing her other hand through the air before her as if wiping clear the world below, including us.

Friday night, Seed stays in to Facetime with a buddy back in Iowa, and the five of us join the growing numbers in the courtyard, up to forty-five or fifty, then fold harnesses into backpacks and head over to Bryant Park, in which we find the same snoozing souls on benches but not a quiver in the trees.

"Must a migrated north," Moses says, and we head further uptown, cross 59th street and enter Central Park, into Hallet Sanctuary, stopping halfway around The Pond.

We scrabble up a rock face and grab a branch, swing ourselves up and see a small platform made of two-by-fours, a launch pad for a zip line clamped around the tree trunk. One at a time, we zip deeper into the trees, gather on the next platform and peer ahead, seeing as our eyes adjust what appears to be a figure hanging upside down, limbs extended at angles like some kind of Vitruvian chick, and further still, a body dropping untethered into a net, bouncing back up into the branches and swinging off, a group materializing to the side, five or six women on a platform twice the size of the one we're on, their figures pulsing in the underwater darkness, moving together in some sort of slow motion dance or maybe tai chi.

"Some kind a dream up here," Smiley says, and we stand in silence until the spell is broken by a zinging sound, a figure flying at us feet first, nearly kicking Moses' head, landing like a paratrooper on the edge of the platform and unclipping from the line.

"What you think you're doin?" It's Hellcat, meanest teacher in the high school.

"We followed you all over from Bryant," I say. "Still just girls?"

"Word you looking for is women," Hellcat says. "What's that make you, boys or men?"

"Shit," Smiley says, and he reaches up, grabs the cable. But before he can lift himself, Hellcat clamps him by the wrist, staring into his face.

"Not if you a child," she says.

"He ain't," Moses says. "Might say some stupid shit but he know better."

"Show me," Hellcat says.

"What?" Smiley says.

"What you know."

Moses unzips his backpack and withdraws his harness. "We been climbing in the courtyard back of these boys' apartments," he says, nodding toward Connie and me.

"I know all about that courtyard," Hellcat says. "Question is, where you think all that climbing gon take you?"

"Right here," I say.

"Oh yeah?" she says, zeroing in on me. "You come to dance with the dickless?"

Not sure how to answer, I look from Hellcat to my boys.

"Huh?" Hellcat says. "This where you mean to be?"

Moses steps forward. "You ain't scaring us off," he says.

Hellcat glares at each of us, one at a time. "Okay then," she says, clipping back onto the line, leaning back against it, widening her stance, "but it's awful dark in there," and she rides off into the trees.

"More nightmare than dream," Smiley says, doubt creeping into his voice, but the rest of us are already moving, Moses sidling over to the tai chi group, his hulking figure absorbed into their slow liquid rhythm, Muzzy and Seed climbing up to a higher zip line, Connie scrabbling past them to the very highest branch, straightening to a stand and swan diving into the open space, tucking as he reaches the net, rolling, bouncing into the opposite stand of trees, darkness closing behind him.

Smiley looks at me, unsure.

"Gotta just go with it," I say.

I lift my shirt over my head, tuck it in my waist, clip on to the line Hellcat took, and I'm gone.

Waking in the afternoon, I hear the television and wander into the den, Lanny today in a grey twill fedora.

"Look who's on the news," he says, Dr. B standing beside a podium behind which is a dude with a white brushback and pin-stripe suit, "NYC School Board Chairman" written across the bottom of the screen.

Chairman steps back and Police Chief steps up, saying they are prepared to do whatever it takes "to bring these kids back into the fold." Next, the City Controller says the Mayor has released ten million dollars from the city's Emergency Fund, and finally it's Bindermaus' turn.

"The key," he says, "is developing new programming in the schools. Otherwise, we will see continued attrition."

"If they're not in school, what are the children doing?" a reporter calls out.

"What children everywhere do," Dr. B says. "Falling through the cracks."

"Gotta watch out for them cracks," Lanny says.

"Maybe we're ascending through em," I say.

"Ascending?" Lanny says. He smiles, shakes his head. "You sound like somebody fixin to climb out a window."

"Courtyard's history," I tell him. "We've been hanging in Central Park, a little farther north each night."

"You going up to Harlem?"

"Far as it takes to get past the lights."

I give Lanny some skin and head out through the door, stashing an extra water bottle with the harness in my backpack, June nights getting warm.

By midnight, must be two hundred of us working new routes in Central Park's North Woods when we hear a loud thunk, a stand of lights blazing into the trees from Central Park West, bodies scrambling for the shadows, scurrying to higher elevations, and we hear Dr. B's voice over a loudspeaker.

"We are here," he says, "because you are valued."

We scamper to a line to take us toward the northern boundary, but when we reach the platform, another stand of lights clunks on from Central Park North, and Hellcat redirects us along a rope course they've set up heading east.

We swing from rope to rope, descend to the ground and cross East Drive, hurry past Harlem Lake, people ahead splitting toward different exits, continue across 5th Avenue and onto Lexington where we catch the number 4 back downtown.

"I'm telling you the same thing I told Consuela Erebus," Bindermaus says from behind his desk, leaning back and to the side, necktie hanging straight as Foucault's pendulum.

"You mean Hellcat," Moses says, sitting beside me on the sofa.

"It's a matter of numbers," he says.

"Chasing us won't bring us back," I say.

"Little man, we've got teachers losing their jobs. Families that don't know where their children are. You've taken this too far."

"We haven't *taken* it anywhere," I say.

"You're unraveling entire communities."

"Then they shouldn't been raveled," Moses says.

Bindermaus walks out from behind the desk, lowers himself into the chair beside the sofa. "We're starting a new program," he says. 'Drop Out-Drop In.' You agree to meet with me and a vocation counselor once a week and we'll give you a bi-weekly stipend of 94 dollars."

"Don't have to do anything? Just have to agree?" I say.

"Yep," he says, returning to his desk, locating a form for each of us, sliding them over for us to sign, which we do.

"Change can't be achieved all at once," he says. "It has to be a process, one step at a time."

"Maybe if you're playing a board game," I say.

Dr. B. pulls in a deep breath, stands and walks to the window. "When I was a junior in college," he says, gazing out toward the slice of sky above the far roofline, "spring term classes ended on Tuesday and finals started the very next day." He glances back to see if we're listening. "Instead of going to finals, the entire student body gathered on the main lawn for three days, giving speeches, chanting, playing music. Our own little 1990s Woodstock."

"So what happened?" I ask.

"They permanently changed the schedule, adding a two-day study period before finals." He turns back to us. "Not saying we changed the world, but we had an effect."

"Sound like you made the semester two days longer," Moses says.

"Because we were improving the system, the quality of the product we were paying for."

"And with the extra two days, they probably raised the price," I say.

"Tuition was going up anyway," he says.

"I'm sure it was," Moses says.

2

Strangest feeling, the air around me solidifying in one particular spot and pressing against my shoulder. I am ascending toward the clouds, rising like vapor toward thin air, but the nudging on my shoulder persists, until finally I wake and see chubby-cheeked Sheila hovering over my bed, open window behind her.

"It's a pufferfish," I say.

"What up, Little Boy?" she says.

"Little Man," I correct.

"Shit," she says.

I make room and she slides under the cover, lays on her back beside me, after a few minutes raising an arm, pointing at the ceiling.

"Orion's belt," she says.

"Sure," I say.

"Them three stars are a thousand light years away."

"How far's that?" I say.

"Didn't you listen in class?" she says. "Farther by the second, everything being pulled away from everything else."

Sheila leans in, wraps both arms around me, hooks her thigh over mine.

"Doesn't feel like you're being pulled away," I say.

"Gravity tryin keep me close," she says, "but that dark energy's always pushing out."

"So we can hook up," I say, "but we'll just get pulled apart."

"That's right," she says, "makes no difference if we do or don't," and she nuzzles her face into my neck, moving up and finding my mouth with hers.

On my way out at dusk, Lanny tells me Cammy, my dad, is on his way to Hell's Kitchen from the Canary Islands where he's been selling Yankee jerseys and Beyonce posters on a beach-side promenade.

Next day, Lanny wakes me at noon, calling me into the den, and there's my dad, wearing a short-brimmed straw fedora, neatly edged white hair beneath it, face leathery and clean-shaven, thick stripes running across his shirt, pin-stripes running down loose navy pants. Looks like some street clown got tangled up with a merchant marine.

Soon as we sit down, my dad says "Oh shit" and skips out to Pablo's, returning with coffee, bagels, and beer, declining Lanny's offer of a ten-spot, and by late afternoon, the two of them are sitting at a table of empty beer cans, trying to get me to join them.

"I flew over three continents and three seasons," my dad says, "just to lay eyes on my own natural born." He takes a long look at me sitting on the sofa. "You're doing fine," he says, "I can see that."

"Quit school and got no job," Lanny chortles. "Damn right he's doing fine!"

"I can see it in your eyes," my father says. "Purpose. Keep following your inner lights, Little Man."

"Okay," I say.

"Don't go chasing no fast money or false promises. Cause in the end, all you got is your inner compass."

"In the beginning too," I say, not seeing how such things change over time.

My father sits there studying me, Lanny beside him looking from him to me, back to him.

"Your grandad used to say, 'Can't pull yourself up by your bootstraps if you ain't got no boots,'" Cammy says.

"Then at the other end," Lanny says, nodding his head, "you got people born on third base thinking they hit a triple."

I go back to bed, rouse at dusk to head out for the night, and wake the next afternoon to Lanny and Cammy's voices, find them in the den, Lanny sitting in his easy chair, my dad standing, butt-nudging the TV stand.

"Yes there is," Lanny says. "What you want and what you got."

"Where you are and where you're going," says Cammy.

"Don't forget where you've been," Lanny says.

"I could never," my father says.

"No difference between em," I say. "You're just a couple of bodies moving through space."

"True true," Lanny says. "That's why you got to roll with things."

"How bout we get us some donuts?" my dad says.

"Pablo's?" Lanny says, and the three of us head out, my dad walking in the middle, bounce-stepping, cheerful, cause he's with his boys, and because he won't be for long.

"Catching that 6:30 flight," he says on the way back, totin a box of Entenmann's cinnamon donuts. "Stopping in Savannah for a couple days, then back to Tenerife."

"What you got in Savannah?" Lanny asks.

"Some dude wants to see my olivine collection."

Lanny shakes his head. "Man could sell a sleigh ride to Santa Claus," he says.

Stopped at a red light on the corner, my father looks at me. "What you think of your old dad?" he says.

"I'm glad."

"Glad what?"

"Glad you got something cooking."

"Cooking *hot*," Lanny says.

My dad reaches over and musses my hair. "You were always like that," he says. "Always gave me the benefit of the doubt."

"Never had any doubt," I say.

"You see?" my father says to Lanny. "You see this son of a bitch? Never had any doubt. I'm going to cut you a big share of the profits, Little Man. Just you wait and see."

By the time we get back and polish off the donuts and a pot of milk and sugar Lanny warms up, it's time for my dad to catch the train to JFK, slinging his satchel over a shoulder, tipping his straw hat forward, and saying with all the fatherly earnestness he can muster, "Always remember, Little Man . . ."

"What?" Lanny says. "Remember what?"

My dad looks at Lanny. "I forgot!" he says.

"That's why you need him to remember!" Lanny bellows.

My dad looks at me and shrugs. Then he tips his hat and hustles off to catch that train.

At dusk, I grab a PB n J, peek in at Lanny nodding in a white fedora with sky blue sash, fighting to stay awake in front of the TV, and head out, take the A train down to Canal Street, walk crosstown to the Manhattan Bridge, evening traffic sliding up onto and down off it, Brooklyn Bridge to my right, half the Williamsburg visible to my left.

That's some serious engineering they got spanning this river. Doesn't accomplish anything, moving people across one way just so they can come back the other, but it's still cool. Well, I think, let's see how tall this Manhattan Bridge is.

I follow the outer walkway to the first tower, climb up a section of girders and find ladder rungs on the Brooklyn side of the tower, scooch it up two-thirds of the way to a small platform, eyeball the Brooklyn Bridge, and in the distance the hazy outline of the granddaddy of them all, the Verrazzano.

"Always looking for a party, ain't you?" It's Hellcat, sitting above me on top of the tower, feet dangling.

"Am I late?" I say.

"Just me over here," she says, and flips on her phone light, waves it, and I follow her gaze over to the Brooklyn Bridge where at the top of the west tower, two lights blink on and jiggle.

"Sheila and Tanika," Hellcat says. "More women on the way."

I pull myself up to the top and sit beside her.

"You traveling solo tonight, Little Man?"

"Checking shit out," I say. "Wondering how much room they got up here."

"The Brooklyn's bigger," she says, tipping her head that way. "Got ladders going up inside the towers, more room on top. But I like this one—" she slaps both hands down on the steel surface beneath her. "And then there's the Williamsburg." Hellcat turns to the Williamsburg Bridge, now in full view, suspension cables strung with lights, headlights flashing along the roadway through cross-hatch girders.

"And if necessary," she says, "I suppose we could take that A train out to the Verrazzano."

"You think?" I say.

"Don't nobody do nothin till they have to."

"But you don't have to."

"I saved up a lot of years, Little Man, living with my mother and her sister, working summers, padding my account. You can spend your whole life tryin fat up, thinking that gon help, gon protect you from something."

Hellcat stands up, walks to the far edge, turns back, performs an exaggerated curtsy, and disappears over the side. Second later, I see her below sliding down a rope, and by the time I get to the bottom, she's a shadow sliding off the bridge, flitting along the water-side walkway toward the Brooklyn.

Next afternoon, I text the boys, and soon's night comes, Moses, Connie, Muzzy, and Seed, still no Smiley, meet me at the base of the Manhattan Bridge's west tower. We free-climb to the first landing and turn to watch a line of figures emerge from the darkness, moving out onto both suspension cables, lugging backpacks filled with gear up onto the towers.

The five of us climb to the top level where four crowning orbs sit like giant closed tulips. Seed eyeballs one and, rangy farm boy he is, grips the steel petals from the underside and pulls himself up, one handhold at a time, settles at the top on his haunches, straddling the pointed tip.

"Can you see Tunisia?" Muzzy calls up.

"I don't climb for the view," Seed says, talking down between his knees.

"I know, right?" Moses says. "Everybody always talking bout the view."

"Tryin get up high where they can look down on shit," Connie says. "Grab that top perch."

"I don't climb to see more," Seed says, "but less," and he tells how back in Center Point he used to climb silos, then the radio tower across from his house where they had this hang-out spot three-quarters of the way up, till one day a kid fell off and died, and how that night at dinner, Seed's dad, who never uttered a word at the table, said, "Maybe now you'll stop your foolishness," and how when two days later his mom broke both legs in a car accident, Seed and his boys disassembled their hang-out platform alright, only instead of lowering it, they moved it up to the top.

"My dad grew so frazzled, my mom decided to send me here to live with her cousin, 'so you can grow up and be somebody,' she said."

I'm mid-zip on the Brooklyn, this one and the Manhattan swarming with bodies, when a search light flashes in my eyes from above, pans over and stops on the east tower, a group of figures scattering. The sound of a second helicopter jacks up the racket, and a second light crosses the first one, scuttles across black water to the Manhattan.

I catch up to Moses on the far side, the first light on us, off us, on us again, and we skitter down and scurry along the walkway to South Street, meet a mob of women coming off the Manhattan who fan out, dispersing into downtown.

3

When someone says my name, I say, "Who?" When they point at me, I look over my shoulder, then back at them. When someone uses a pronoun, any one at all, I have a split moment of doubt—"What's that?" I say.

"Little Man."

"Huh?

"It's me, Muzzy."

"Muzzy?"

"Are you sleeping up here?"

"No, man, just sitting."

I'm on the top of the first tower of the Verrazzano. Saw a figure up here, thought it was Sheila, but just as I reached the top, it slipped away.

When someone leaves, it's like a door opening, unblocking the view, so instead of looking at her, I'm peering out into the night, to the lit-up Statue of Liberty, the sparkling high rises of Jersey City, and the ones downtown, Freedom Tower rising up between them.

"Seed has left," Muzzy says.

But I'm trying to wrap my head around the sheer mass of those buildings, all those pinpricks of light pushing out into the night, the way they look far away and close up at the same time, wondering how space actually works, where it goes when it gets filled in with shit.

"Little Man."

"Yeah?"

"He is returning to Iowa."

A hazy sliver of pink light appears on the horizon over Long Island. The rosy fingers of dawn—who said that?

"I need to go after him," Muzzy says. "The situation in Iowa is not good."

I look at Muzzy's worried face. "When did he split?" I ask.

"One hour ago. Maybe one hour and a half. Said he had money for a bus."

I withdraw my phone, check the bus schedules to Iowa. "One leaving now, changes in Detroit. Another one in two hours, changes in Cleveland. You might catch him at Port Authority."

"I will go," Muzzy says.

"Keep me posted," I say.

"Posted? Send you letters?"

"Text me, dude."

Muzzy smiles. "Of course," he says.

"You have money?" I say.

"Some."

I take out my wallet, hand him what's left from the first city check I cashed two days earlier, 86 dollars, plucking back a five for the subway, then, changing my mind, push the five back into his hand.

Tonight, those chicks are going hard, marching like soldiers up Dead Man Hill, humping their gear up the Verrazzano's east side suspension cable, ribbon of headlights on the Belt Parkway stretching into the distance behind them.

"Y'all doing some Trail of Tears shit!" I call from atop the first tower, my voice barely reaching them through the wind and rising noise of traffic. "Bunch of Syrian refugees! Carrying all your worldly belongings!"

Hellcat appears on the tower surface, sets down her pack, walks toward me, leaving the other girls dropping ropes, connecting ziplines, crossways and down.

"Can't you see we workin, Little Man?" Hellcat says

"Working like Sisyphus," I say.

"Really?" she says. "This what you bringing tonight, mockery?" Hellcat sits beside me. "Something eatin you, boy?"

"We lost two—Seed and Muzzy."

"So now you the one keeping count?" Hellcat says.

I point toward a couple lights bobbing above the Hudson. "Bindermaus and them gonna be here soon."

"Oh, they coming," she says, "they always coming. Meantime, we got to get us heads up where we can breathe. Now, how bout you help us set up this super-recoil bungee cord?"

"Super recoil?"

"It's time to party, Little Man. Like it's 1999. Like now it's 2019, it's *really* 1999."

"Cause we living on borrowed time," I say.

"Only kind there is," Hellcat says.

Sheila appears at my side, her warm arm pressing against mine for a moment, then she turns and looks at me, eyes peering out from round face, dead level with mine.

"Damn," she says, "you losing more height?"

"Must a run off with your cheek bones," I say, and the three of us set to work installing wire rope clips to affix the bungee cord.

Hellcat and Sheila move to opposite sides of the tower, each walk fifty feet or so down their respective suspension cables, Sheila tossing a weighted line clear across, lasso style, to Hellcat who loops it around the cable and ties it off.

Back on the surface of the tower, Hellcat harnesses up, clips onto the bungee cord, and I spread my arms and announce, "Ladies and Gentlemen! The one and only, gravity-defying, Hellcat Erebus!"

Hellcat tugs the cord to make sure it's secure. "What goes down must come up," she says.

Hellcat steps forward and freefalls toward the seven lanes of thinning traffic, cord extending to its full length and snapping her back up, all the way to where she grabs with both hands the line they tied across, then shimmies over, swings under and up onto the cable, walks back to the top, unclipped bungee cord in hand.

Sheila goes next, bounces back up even higher, flying over and around the cross line, catapulting back to us atop the tower, landing on her feet.

"I'll show you how to party," I say.

I take the end of the line from Sheila but, not wearing my harness, release it so it clanks and topples off the steel surface. "No sense going one way just so you can come back the other," I say.

"Don't worry," Hellcat says to Sheila, "we lose this one, gon pick up plenty others."

"Who's keeping count now?" I call back, then turn to Sheila. "You need to tell Hellcat about that dark energy."

Sheila steps toward me, her eyes glinting faintly in the distant light. "I seen some crazy motherfuckers," she says.

"Only crazy if you try to pin us down," I say.

Just then, a jet taking off from JFK thunders over the harbor behind me, and I turn away from the women, the women whom we are forever falling behind and overtaking, falling behind and overtaking, the three of us standing still watching the jet rise, its roar trailing after in its wake, that regal lady down there, reaching with her torch as it climbs toward the darkness.

4

I didn't jump—didn't have to. Letting go isn't a one-time thing, it's a principle, a law of physics—entropy, dispersal, dark energy—something that takes time.

Next day, Lanny comes in and wakes me—Sheila had spotted me two-fifty for the train home—and I glance at the window, assessing the weather. Overcast, mid-afternoon, early June."

"You have a visitor," Lanny says. "Mr. Psychology Man."

"Bindermaus?"

"Don't know about no mouses," Lanny says. "But the dude is wearing some kind of sweat suit, like he on his way to the gym, so you bes not keep him waiting."

I pull on my jeans, worn and soft from not being washed, grab a hoodie, find Dr. B standing in the den beside the dummies.

"You haven't completed your half of our bargain," he says.

"All I had to do was agree."

"Agree to meet with me and a second counselor."

"And I did, I agreed. No, no, man, I did my part."

"Little man," Dr. B says, "agreeing doesn't just mean making a promise. It means keeping it."

"That's *not* what agreeing means. It means saying okay, dude, I *agree* to do that."

"You're getting hung up on the literal meaning of the words," Dr. B says, "ignoring the spirit of them."

"Spirit? Now, you're definitely buggin." I take a tan fedora with a yellow sash off a dummy. "If I flip this hat toward you—" I fling it backhand, and he catches it against his chest—"there ain't no spirit. I'm just tossing a fedora."

"But you intended for me to catch it. There was an implicit transaction."

"Nah. I was curious to see what you'd do, but I had no intention at all, other than to throw it. Y'all get too caught up in transactions, trying to control people, doing something so they'll do something."

Dr. B returns the hat to the dummy's head. "Looks like we're right back where we started."

"Where else we gonna be?" I say.

When you're conceived at the end, where there's simply no more room, you only have one way to go. It's no longer about gravity and shit pressing down—no, gravity's finished its work—but about dark energy pushing out, away.

I was twelve, still living with my mom in the Bronx, when I first pieced together the date of my conception, September 10, or more likely, early morning, September 11, 2001.

My mother had sunk into a deep depression and I'd sat up with her at night, making tea, talking.

"Our last night together, your father and I went to a late movie at the Bronx Plaza," she said, "came back to my room, drank wine and ate pizza. The next morning, he headed off to the West Village to sell his jewelry off a blanket, and that afternoon, as I sat watching the footage of those buildings coming down, he called from New Jersey, saying he'd seen the plane hit the first tower, hopped the train to Newark to pick up his Aerostar, and was heading to Florida.

"He'd served in Iraq with Uncle Lanny," she said, "only he'd stayed on after Lanny was sent home. Then the war came chasing him to New York, and all he could do was run."

For a long time, she said, she mistook his running for fear—of his past, of her, of being a father—but only because she herself was afraid, of losing him, of being left with a responsibility, a child, she knew she couldn't handle.

"When buildings start falling, Little Man," she said, "and you're already living on borrowed time, you'd be a fool to stick around."

The next winter my mom and I moved again, like reverse underground railroad refugees, white mother and child (my dad was Columbian but more white than brown) being sheltered by a network of tias and aunties and amoos, first to Tia Munello's apartment on East 141st in the Bronx where we slept on air mattresses in a corner of the living room behind sheets hanging from a clothesline, then to Morris Avenue into a bedroom with a standing partition we shared with Amoo Feeren, a silent thickset woman from Iran who took in laundry, washing it in a machine in her kitchen and hanging it to dry on four lines with pulleys extending out the back window.

Couple days before I left the Bronx, I was on my way home from school and some dude was making a scene in the subway station, yelling and screaming how he was going to jump in front of a train, zeroing in on a woman in a head scarf, stepping toward her.

"Look at me!" he shouted. "If you can't look at yourselves, look at me!"

People stood by, a couple calling 911, others watching to see how the scene would play out, the woman slowly backpedaling until the guy turned his attention to someone else, the person retreating, and I stepped up.

The guy's eyes bored into me. "You want to die today, young fella?"

"No," I answered.

"Then you better run!" the dude roared. "I hear that train coming!"

"Where?" I asked him. "Run where?"

"Home, boy! Run home to your mama!"

"I'm already going home," I said, not understanding his logic.

"Not if I pull you under that train you ain't!"

I listened a moment, along with the others standing by, but the tunnels both ways were silent.

Dude stepped close, face etched with deep creases, and I could see he'd been feeling this way for a while—I wasn't the first person he'd wanted to murder. A zephyr of warm air issued from the tunnel and I heard the distant rumble of a train. The guy reached out and grabbed my shoulder.

"You ready to die?" he said.

"If it's my time," I said, still pretty sure it wasn't.

Dude eyed me another moment, then spun away. "You people have to make up your minds!" he hollered. "Choose—life or death!"

As the train burst from the tunnel, the guy straightened, offered a polite bow, turned back to the track, and jumped.

That night as I lay in bed, I thought about the dude, about living and dying, and about a question I had asked in class about why north was up and south down, teacher saying she didn't know, was just how they decided to do it.

"So it could have been the other way around," I said.

"Yeah," she said with a shrug, head drooping, shoulders caving, same as every teacher I'd had, "I suppose everything could have been."

5

I scoop Connie from his apartment, and we tool on over to the playground on 10ᵗʰ Avenue, sitting against the fence watching Moses, Smiley, couple other dudes from the team playing 5-on-5 against a collection of older dudes, couple of them ex-high school stars.

"Yeah, Mosey!" Connie calls out after Moses muscles the opposing big dude aside and drops a deuce. "Them has-beens can't touch you!"

Moses glances over, jogging back up the court, next time on offense missing a jumper from the top of the key.

"Get back in that paint, boy!" Connie calls. "Show these skeletons what time it is!"

But Moses doesn't have any zip, summer heat kicking in, batteries running low.

Other point guard leads the break up the court, Smiley going for the steal, not even coming close, dude glancing back at him, laughing.

"Next time, Smiles," Connie calls, 'you take the ball *and* his social security check!"

Connie's like a white lab born into a litter of black puppies, no idea he's a different color, been friends with these guys since he was a toddler.

Game ends, older dudes wander off, and Connie trots out, hoists up a long shot that clangs off the rim, returns to sit with us against the fence.

"Don't know about this shit," Moses says.

"You get em next time, cuz," Connie says.

"Getting hotter every day," Smiley says.

"Ain't the heat," Moses says. "It's like we rolling around in a box. Hit one side and go right back to the other."

"Tomorrow," Connie says, "you pump your asses full of electrolytes, come out here, and kick some ass."

"Or not," I say, the three of them looking at me as I walk over, pick up the basketball. Cupping it in my wrist, I take aim and whip it high into the air, over the hoop, over the fence, ball disappearing into the darkness beyond.

"Might be time to cross that Verrazzano," I say.

Back at Lanny's, I pack up my gear, stuff in some extra boxers and socks, portable phone charger, roll the army blanket from my bed up tight and attach it with the cords on the bottom of the backpack. I text the boys do the same, everyone responding with an affirmative except Smiley, who asks a bunch of questions I don't bother answering. Then I post an Instagram for our growing list of followers: "Pack an overnight bag, y'all."

On my way out, I stop in the den where Lanny's sitting in a powder blue fedora with orange flower sash watching a Mets game, tell him I might be gone a while.

Lanny turns from the TV, gives me the once over, offers a sleepy smile. "The walkin's good," he says, "and the road ain't crowded."

* * *

We're chilling on the Verrazzano's west tower near Staten Island, line of kids behind us extending back to the east tower, and farther, to where bodies are still filing out of the A-train station, pre-dawn traffic calm, couple hovering dragon flies with search lights over by Ellis Island.

Finally, Moses says we need to bust this move, hoists on his backpack and starts down the suspension cable.

"Not like they gon get lost," he says over his shoulder. "Only one way to go."

"Where?" Smiley asks. "Go where?"

"Check out a couple of these famous Staten Island parks," I say.

"Only made those parks cause nobody want to live there," Connie says, humping his pack behind Smiley.

"Got some rednecks want to," Moses calls back.

We reach the end of the cable and lower ourselves with ropes down the concrete stanchion, drop our backpacks, and jump onto the sandy strand.

In my whole life, I've been to Staten Island one time, when my dad was in town, going to see a dude wanted to buy some jade. Now we're walking up South Beach, sun rising in the east over Coney Island, till Moses drops his backpack, unties his blanket and, without a word, curls up in the sand, rest of us following suit, dudes behind us dropping their packs wherever they are, settling down and going to sleep, dudes in the distance still jumping down from the bridge.

In the afternoon, I wake to see a couple of moms with their kids splashing in the water, still too early for the summer crowds, four dudes leaning on the railing of the boardwalk. I roll up my blanket, pull on my sneakers, and when I look back more dudes have joined the four. I nudge Moses awake, Connie joining us with his loaded backpack.

"Who they?" Moses says.

"Staten Island rednecks," Connie says.

"Hang on," I say, and walk over to the dudes at the railing.

"What's this," one dude says to me, "some kind of invasion?" He's wearing light blue stone-washed jeans and a paisley shirt, sleeves rolled up to his elbows.

"You them boys quit school?" another says, this guy stocky, wearing blue-jean shorts reach past his knees.

"Wouldn't say quit," I say, "cause we were never part of it." I turn and look down the stretch of beach leading back to the bridge, see dudes collecting their stuff and moving up over the boardwalk railing, seeking points of egress. "One of y'all got a cigarette?" I ask.

Dude in long shorts reveals a pack, flips open the top, and I take one. A third dude steps over with a light, and I suck in, quickly releasing the smoke before I cough.

"Where they going?" dude in paisley shirt says.

"To check out your parks, find some trees," I say. "We do better off the ground."

"Latourette's got the most," Long Shorts says, "but High Rock's good too."

"And Blood Root," says Paisley Shirt. "Compared to that concrete jungle—" he nods toward Brooklyn and Manhattan— "must seem like you're out in the boonies."

"Out where we can breathe," I say.

"Oh, we can breathe alright," says Long Shorts.

I offer my hand to Long Shorts to shake and he clasps my thumb, homie style, with a finger slide and snap, other three doing the same. Whitest dudes I've ever seen shaking hands like the brothers.

I walk back, tell my boys the rednecks are chill, and we pull on our backpacks and head inland, breaking into parts, like any mass oozing around obstacles, moving toward the greenbelt looking for trees, come to a sign says Latourette one way and Blood Root Valley the other. Moses doesn't ask, just leads toward Blood Root.

"What you waitin for?" I say, coming up on Moses, stopped, peering up into a big leafy maple.

Moses doesn't move, just keeps looking up toward the soft hum of pulley on cable and clanking metal. I jump up, grab the lowest branch, pull myself up to a sit, see a body above flit across open space releasing a dark spray, and hear a call sounds like a raptor. Then another body passes at a different angle, and I feel cool mist on my face, female voice calling out, "Let er go, ladies!" and in rapid fire two figures trailing dark veils of vapor cross the opening, and two more on a higher line, another one higher still, bodies whooshing back the other way, more mist coating my face and shoulders.

"From the tippy top branches clear down to the roots, ladies!" calls a voice. "We fertilizin the world!"

Moses points out two white girls sitting up above, must be Staten Islanders, one of them holding in her hands a large jug, tipping it and pouring dark liquid into a cannister with a spray nozzle held by the other, who seals it closed and hands it off to a third who glides down the line releasing a veil of spray.

"You shouldn't be here, Little man!" a voice calls down, sounds like Sheila. "This a woman's party!"

I lower myself back to the ground where Moses and I look at each other's faces. I run a finger across his cheek and show it to him.

"Red rain," he says.

"Blood," I say. "Blood Root Valley."

Moses dabs his own cheek, licks his finger. "Cranberry Juice," he says. "Them chicks bleedin cranberry juice."

We slap hands and slog off toward Latourette Park, dudes already up ahead, dismantling park benches, hammering in landing platforms, cables, pulleys, attaching fine-mesh landing nets somebody brought.

In the wee hours, girls migrate over from Blood Root, partner up with whomever they can, Sheila squeezing into my hammock, saying she finally got to see what that Blood Root thing was about, how they'd heard about the gatherings but couldn't ever make it over.

"Like Staten Island a million miles away," I say.

"One or a million," she says, "sometimes hard to tell."

Other girls migrating over, teaching boys stunts, swinging from their arms, flipping onto the landing platforms, diving in dual-twirling corkscrews down between the branches into nets, Hellcat and others moving out ahead to set up new lines, other pairs creeping off, nestling together in hammocks made from blankets or sleeping bags.

Connie and a few others head to a nearby 24-hour Walmart, returning with batteries for phone chargers, loaves of bread, jars of peanut butter and jelly, plastic utensils which, after eating, we lick clean and stash in our backpacks.

We wake late afternoon, women gone, lay there bullshitting as the sun sinks low, then pack up and move out, reaching platforms the women built in trees along the river in Clay Pit Pond and, as dusk closes in, stop and gaze up at the Outerbridge Crossing, the last few female figures on the far side sliding down into Jersey.

"Now where we goin?" Smiley asks.

"Going west, young man," I say.

"Just like them girls," Moses says.

"Word you looking for is women," I say.

"Word I'm looking for is hos," Moses says.

"Better watch it," I say, "Hellcat'll come back and kick your ass."

"Oooh," Connie says, "she can kick mine first."

"Ain't nothin in Jersey," Smiley says.

"How you know?" Moses says. "You ain't ever been."

"That's *why* I never been. Jersey come to New York. New York don't go to Jersey."

"Damn Muzzy," Connie mutters, staring at his phone. "Dumb ass got stuck in Pittsburgh," he says, raising his head. "I Venmoed him money to go from Harrisburg to Cedar Rapids, but he missed the transfer."

"Need to do a fundraiser for that boy," Moses says.

"Get him some Seed money," I say.

"I started a GoFundMe fore we left Latourette," Connie says. "Already got three hundred dollars."

"I saw that shit," Smiley says. "What you mean, 'hashtag Unseeding America'?"

"I mean three hundred dollars in the last two hours. Making my next post now: 'CantJoinUsFundUs'."

"Yo!" a voice calls from below.

Down on the ground we see Paisley Shirt and Long Shorts, wearing backpacks, Long Shorts sporting a hoodie with a confederate flag on the chest.

"We're going with you," Paisley Shirt says. "We got gear and money."

We drop our packs to the ground, then ourselves, a whole crowd of white dudes with backpacks at the edge of the lawn.

"People gon do what they gon do," Moses says, humpin his pack past me toward the bridge, rest of us falling in behind him, Staten Island dudes too, some breaking off to join another group on the shore below the bridge, Moses reaching the cement stanchion, free climbing up, crawling on all fours along the steep surface till he reaches the wall running along the roadway, where he slowly rises up onto two feet, evolving like homo erectus on a timeline, tightroping along, arms out to either side, toward the steel trusses bracing the center sections of the bridge.

At the top of the first cantilevered peak, we settle down and take in the view, beneath us dark forms swinging and climbing, some setting up ropes to traverse Tarzan style, others arm-swinging girder to girder, while out on the river, a flotilla of black dots passes across the water, kids on rafts made from shipping pallets, branches, surface shimmering in the lights from the bridge and waterside industry.

"Yo!" Hanging one-armed from a steel truss, Long Shorts grins over at us.

"Good thing you wearing that Dixie flag," Moses calls to him.

"Brings me luck," he answers, missing the sarcasm, swinging himself to the next truss, Paisley Shirt close behind, other Staten Island boys scattered about, absorbing into the mix.

As the night deepens, I climb to the top of Outerbridge Crossing, breathing deep the night air, the weight of daytime draining from my body, red and yellow lights of the New Jersey treatment plants on one side, pale tones of Staten Island's waterfront on the other. I think about Lanny, then my dad, my mom, note how the darkness opens up the world, releasing us to pursue the next ascent, the next forest, pheromones, before the sun overtakes us, reaching after us with its rosy fingers—who the hell said that?—grabbing hold of us as it passes over, slips beyond the edge, releasing us back into the night.

6

Connie stamps his feet against the metal surface of the huge gas tank we crashed on, waking us, announcing the GoFundMe account has surpassed five thousand dollars, kids donating from Massachusetts to D.C.

"I'm tweetin out my cell number for any westward-crawlin motherfucker needs a dime," he says. "Had to deputize couple dudes in different states, made em regional treasurers. Youngbloods needin sleeping bags and phone chargers."

Once they landed in Jersey, kids started hitching rides, some with 18-wheelers at the A1 Truck Stop, others taking Amtrak, Rideshare, once word got out we had funds.

Soon as night falls, we start seeing posts from wherever dudes get dropped—flash-illuminated photos of kids swinging from shut-down chairlifts in the Poconos, swarming over fire towers in the national forest, one salt and pepper group—Staten Island kids mixed with Guyanese and Trinidadian dudes, probably from Ozone Park in Queens—stringing cables from the spires across Main Street in the town of Jim Thorpe, camera flashes carving out small caves of light in the darkness.

Bout midnight, batch of posts appears from Hershey Park, the Ferris wheel and roller coaster strung with ropes and cables, video clips showing dudes on different levels, one of Paisley Shirt swinging from a horizontal cable, releasing into a full layout rotation, disappearing into the leaves of a nearby tree, my boys and me, meantime, tracking the scent of the girls, the *women*, Sheila dropping posts like breadcrumbs, "Best Thai food in Allentown," "Why capitol cities always so ugly?", us catching a ride west the following morning in a big-rig petroleum truck, driver making room in the sleeping compartment, putting on fresh pillow cases, taking us two at a time beside him in the cockpit.

Chunky dude with a lime-green baseball cap says, PA GAS CO, driver tells us he's got to make a stop on the way in Sex Town.

"They got brothels in Pennsylvania?" Connie says.

"Just the nickname we gave the place," driver says. "Actual name is Intercourse."

"Better drop us on the highway," Smiley says.

"Shut up," Moses says. "Probably mean intercourse like talking to people."

"They say it's because it's where the two main roads, 340 and 772, converge," driver says. "But I'm not convinced. It's an old Amish town, and once you see the number of children they have per family, I believe you'll share my skepticism."

We pull into a gas station on the edge of the village, driver telling us give him an hour to fill the tanks, and we continue on foot into town, Connie and Smiley pulling 360s when a horse and buggy clops past.

We come to an A-frame sign on the sidewalk says "Emma's Shoofly Pie," and walk into a courtyard beneath an inscribed arch: *Amish Country: Where Good Things Stay Good.*

We grab a patio table at the Harvest Café, woman about thirty in a white apron bringing us menus.

"You like Intercourse?" Connie says to her.

"We're here for some shoofly pie," Moses says quickly.

"Which would you like first?" waitress says, eyeing Connie.

Connie turns to me. "Amish chick with some sass," he says.

"You're right about the sass," waitress says, "which makes you half right. Half more than usual, I'm guessing."

"If you ain't Amish, why you workin here?" Moses says.

Waitress shakes her head. "How many slices, four?" she says.

"Five," Smiley says, shooting an apologetic glance to Moses.

Waitress brings us the pie, Smiley's plate with two slices, and a minute later returns with a pitcher of milk and four glasses, three of them regular, fourth an oversized goblet for Smiley.

"Someday I'm gonna come back and marry that chick," Smiley says, mouth filled with pie, pouring milk from the pitcher into his goblet.

Waitress returns Connie's credit card with the receipt and asks where we're from.

"New York City," Connie says.

"Some kind of school trip?" she asks.

"Came on our own," Moses says.

"Why here?"

"Where the truck we ridin with stopped," says Moses.

"Well," waitress says, "you want to meet an Amish person, follow me."

Smiley forks the last piece of pie into his mouth, and we follow her down the steps over a small lawn to another building, furniture shop, filled with bed frames, tables, chairs, some bare wood, others with a satiny finish.

"Daniel," the waitress says to a man at a desk, "these boys are having trouble telling who's Amish."

Daniel's got a light brown beard in an arc around his jaw, no mustache. Waitress goes back to the restaurant, and Daniel comes out from behind the desk, shakes our hands, asks each of us about our family back home. When it comes out that we quit school, he says his son, Daniel Jr, also quit, that school oftentimes leads young people astray.

He says Daniel Jr is working in the woodshop at home now and that if we'd like to pay a visit, he's about to go home for lunch.

Connie and I jog back to the gas station to check with the driver, who says another hour is no problem, he needs to get some lunch himself, and we pile into Daniel's buggy parked behind the shop, horse wearing blinders, facing into a stand of trees.

"Just like they got in Central Park," Smiley says.

"Only this one takin you someplace," Moses says.

"Yeah, back in time," Connie says.

"Backward, forward," I say. "Ain't no difference."

Four of us squeeze into the cabin behind the driver's seat, ten minutes later climb out before an unpainted barn beside a white clapboard house with a neatly-edged stone pathway, Daniel leading us into the barn to meet his son, looks about our age.

"Where's your beard, dude?" Connie asks him.

Junior glances at his dad, then says, "We don't grow them until after marriage."

Moses scratches the scruff on his chin, glances at the rest of our patchy three-day growths, mine barely visible.

Dad tells Junior we're here to see the woodshop, goes to the house for lunch, and Junior leads us over to a freshly made mahogany dresser.

"All our work is done in the traditional manner," Junior says.

"What your dad was saying about stayin where you are, stead of movin around," Smiley says.

"On a planet flying through space at ten thousand miles an hour," I say, "makes sense to hold on to what you can."

"Yes it does," Junior says.

"That's why we got these things," Connie says, showing his phone. "It's like a modern day compass, helps us stay on course."

"You have one?" Smiley asks Junior.

"No," he says.

"This little device," Connie says, "can tell you anything you want to know. Hold on," he says, thumbing the keys, peering down at his screen. "Did you know Mount Everest is twenty-nine thousand, twenty-nine feet tall, and the temperature right now in Kathmandu is twenty-two degrees?"

"Celsius," I say.

Connie works his phone another second. "Twenty-two Celsius, seventy-one Fahrenheit."

Dude nods politely though clearly is not impressed. His father appears in the doorway, and Moses steps over, gives Junior a bro-hug, rest of us doing the same.

"Stay safe," Junior calls as we file toward the door.

"You stay safe," Moses says, turning back, winking. "We goin the other way. We goin to Kathmandu."

7

"Fix them buttons," Smiley says.

Moses fastens two brass buttons on his gray overcoat. "How'd we end up with the Confederacy?" he asks.

"Last day of the battle," Smiley says, "and they losin numbers."

"And cause all these volunteers want to be union soldiers," I say, four of us in a farmhouse basement with a bunch of older dudes pulling on gray uniforms.

Truck driver's next stop after Intercourse turned out to be a gas station beside the Gettysburg Battlefield. He pulled in off the highway, told us there was a McDonalds on the other side of the cemetery back of the station, gave us 90 minutes.

Must have taken the wrong route through the cemetery cause we came out at the entrance to the National Military Park, figured they must have a concession, paid the student fee and walked in. Inside a restored farmhouse, instead of food, we found a group of big-bellied men in various states of undress, dude with a red beard asking us where the hell we came from, then saying never mind, they're running low on Confederates, tossing us each a matching gray coat and trousers from a pile.

"They got doctors and lawyers on that side," another bearded dude complains, "and what do we get, couple skinny kids."

"One of em got some size," guy with bushy stache and sideburns says, nodding toward Moses. "Why aren't you boys in school?" he asks. "Summer vacation don't start for another week."

"Field trip," Moses answers.

"We used to take a lot of field trips," says another dude, sitting on a bench pulling on a pair of infantry boots, must be his own.

"Yeah," says the dude with the stache, "we'd take a tab of LSD and spend the day out in a field!"

"You guys get paid to do these re-enactments?" Connie asks.

"Hell no," dude says. "Hank there got no choice. Community service requirement for a reduced sentence. Rest of us are here so we don't forget."

"Don't forget what?" asks Connie.

"The bloodshed," says the dude, stooping to fingernail-brush his stache in a mirror on the wall. "The waste," he says, "the carnage."

"You know what they say about history," says another dude, this one tall and slim, clean shaven. "If you don't learn it, you're doomed to repeat it."

"Though it might work the other way," I say. "Learning it *makes* you repeat it."

Dude stares over at me a few seconds, and dips back down to pull on his second boot.

Wool coats and pants are so big we wear them over our clothes, Moses too, without even taking off our sneakers, cinch the trousers tight with twine, follow the men out to a supply shed, each of us grabbing a musket and pouch of ammo, and tromp out to the battlefield where some colonel on a horse, barking orders, waving a sword, lines us up along one edge of the field.

"Load muskets!" the colonel shouts, and we do what the others do, tearing open a pouch with our teeth, pouring the powder into the barrel, then detaching the ramrod and packing it in.

"Don't worry," I say to Smiley, "there's no lead ball, just powder."

"Forward march!" calls the colonel.

Shoulder to shoulder we proceed toward a line of union soldiers, advancing from across the way.

"Company halt!" Colonel prances out before us on his horse. "Load muskets!"

"Already loaded em, Dave," someone calls to the colonel.

An explosion of shots erupts from the union soldiers about a hundred yards away, and three of our guys drop to the ground.

"Takin it for the team," Connie, beside me, says, another round of blasts released from the bluecoats, broken into two squads taking turns, two more of our Confederates moaning and falling.

"What the fuck?" Moses says at Connie's other shoulder. "I got to die so others can live?"

"Live?" Connie says. "You dyin so these reenactment motherfuckers can die again. And again."

"Nah man," Moses says. "I'm out of here."

Moses tosses his rifle aside, turns back and makes a run for it, other three of us taking off after him.

"Deserters!" cries the colonel. "Infantry, about face!"

Over my shoulder, I see the line of men pivot back with their loaded muskets, take aim as we weave across the field, making ourselves difficult to target.

"Fire!" the colonel cries, muskets exploding, Smiley diving and rolling, bouncing up, regaining the rest of us as we reach the supply house and duck in a side door.

We dump our coats and trousers, and when we exit the other side, the colonel spots us, takes off after us at a gallop, leaving his infantry behind, the four of us making it to a stand of trees, swinging up and into a large maple, the colonel dancing about on his horse below.

"Come down and face justice!" he shouts. "You cannot desert! Especially you young ones, upon whom our fates depend!"

We climb up high, deep into the cover of leaves, spot the colonel down there skipping this way and that, unsure which way we've gone.

Once the coast is clear, we descend and double back to the gas station, the big rig gone, find our backpacks lined up beside a small island with an air pump and coin-operated vacuum, then head back to the trees, where we follow the afternoon sun, picking our way west through the few acres of forest, descend to cross a broad field, and head up into the next stand of trees, hop-scotching from field to trees till we reach the Michaux State Forest, which Connie reports has nothing but mountains and trees for miles.

At sunset, we tie our blankets and sleeping bags to branches, share a jar of peanut butter and some rolls, only sounds the rustling leaves and a few cheeping birds.

"Nothing better," Moses says, holding up the plastic jar in the last of the day's light filtering through the leaves. He opens his water bottle, takes a long pull. "Ahhhhhh."

"Like them arranged marriages they got in India," Smiley says.

"Say what?" Moses says.

"Less is more," I say. "Like the Amish back there in Intercourse."

"What my mom always sayin when I was a kid," Connie says. "'Get what you get and don't get upset.'"

"That the same mom got caught cheatin on your pops?" Moses says.

"Point is to get back to basics," Smiley says. "Take away the extra options, shit taste better."

"Nah man," Moses says, "once you give em options, you can't take em back. That more-option genie come out the bottle pretty easy but you *never* get that motherfucker back in."

"That's why we're up here," I say, "where everything tastes better."

"Where them soldiers can't get us," Smiley says.

"Which side you talkin bout?" Connie asks him.

"Both. They both tryin kill us."

"Nah man," Connie says, gazing out through the leaves at the darkening sky, sun sinking low, leaves hanging still, "we good up here in Kathmandu."

I wake in the darkness, a moon blinking above a stirring breeze, see Smiley and Connie's hammocks empty, Moses beside me on his back, blank face basting in the moonlight, eyelids lightly fluttering. Beyond him, I see a figure drop from a branch, grab onto one below, another body dropping after it, then another.

Dark figures scamper up a trunk further out, one after another, then drop through the darkness onto lower branches, landing and springing forward, swinging one-armed, closest one clasping the arm of the next, swinging body to body, melting away into the night.

8

The four of us emerge from the forest into the town of Pond Bank, stock up on food and water at a convenience store, sneak into the back of a delivery truck for a company from Pittsburgh, hearing the driver's voice through the partition, telling dispatch he'll be at Somerset in an hour and a half, Pittsburgh an hour after that.

At Somerset, driver opens the back doors and nearly faints when Smiley greets him—"What up, bro?"

Dude, can't be 30 years old, gives us a talking to, not about stowing away but about scaring people, saying it's the ones who do the unexpected shit that are screwing up the world.

We skulk off stoop-shouldered, watch from the sidewalk as the driver returns to the van, replaces the hand truck, closes the back doors, and as soon as he heads back into the store with his clipboard, we scoot over and climb back in.

Van empty except for a couple boxes, four of us stretch out in the darkness, driver starting the motor and whisking us toward Pittsburgh. Then we hear the driver's voice, getting louder, arguing with someone.

"Goddammit!" he shouts, words coming clearly into the back. "What the hell is so important that you cannot do this for me?"

He's quiet a minute, then we barely hear him say, "This is the last time I will ask."

Then again, a moment later, his voice breaking. "Betsy, I'm begging you."

We lay quiet, listening, till we hear his voice. "Lewis, it's me. I'm done with texting. Just want you to know I love you."

We feel the van ascend an incline, then stop, Connie checking his phone, saying we're on the Fort Duquesne Bridge in Pittsburgh. Moses cracks the rear door and peeks out, rest of us at his shoulder, river spreading out on one side, streaked with light from the shore, cars stopping behind us, whizzing past us one lane over, Moses tilting his head back, looking up.

"Like the Outerbridge," he says.

"This one's bowstring-arch," I say, gazing at the arched ceiling of criss-crossing girders.

Driver's door opens and thunks closed.

"Not sure bout this dude," Moses says, and we file out the back, traffic backing up behind us.

Sitting on the steel barrier beside the walkway, driver sees us approaching and starts shimmying up a vertical cable.

"Home boy got some skill," Connie says.

"Nothin a body can't do once it give up," Moses says, and the four of us set to worming our way up the cables.

Hundred or so feet above the roadway, we reach the arcing trusses, see the driver sitting out in the center at the highest point, hoist ourselves up to rest, dark bowl of the football stadium on one shore, downtown Pittsburgh sparkling against a black velvet backdrop on the other.

A pack of kids, must be local, ascends the vertical cables on the other side, at the top one of them hooking his legs over a girder and hanging upside down, next one lowering a rope, sliding down beside the first dude and latching onto his hands, unfolding into a ladder, four more kids sliding down, adding themselves to the chain, tucking, untucking, rocking into lengthening arcs.

"We told you we'd be up here," one of the kids calls to the driver.

"They must know this dude," Smiley says.

"I mean it this time!" driver calls to them.

"That's why we're here, asshole!" kid calls back.

"That and to try out their new gear from that GoFundMe," Connie says.

"Let's give em some backup," Moses says, and he hooks his knees over a girder and reaches down toward the roadway, swings up and clasps hands with Connie who flips down, then swings his feet up for me, then me for Smiley, four of us descending our own chain.

Alone on the peak of the cross-bow cage, the driver begins inching his way down the arch.

"Jump this way!" a Pittsburgh dude calls, but the driver keeps moving toward the edge.

"Who's Betsy?" Connie calls to him.

"My wife," driver says, just loud enough for us to hear.

"And Lewis?" calls Smiley.

"My son."

"Dude raveled alright," Moses says.

"Jump this way!" I call, our chain rocking into motion.

Couple feet before the edge of the cage, driver stops, seems to exhale, deflate a little, shoulders relaxing, tilts his head back to the empty sky above and falls backward, arms floating out to the side as he drops toward the roadway, our chain swinging in from one side, chain of Pitt kids from the other, Smiley catching one arm while the bottom Pitt kid grabs the other, the two chains locking together in a V, connected by the driver who hangs peaecefully in our arms.

9

Last post from Sheila saying something about the biggest bowl of ketchup she's ever seen, we find a walkway along the bridge's lower level, continue past a steady trickle of kids coming the other way, some wearing harnesses, couple with coils of cable over their shoulders, extending hands as they pass, a mix of dudes and chicks, coming to join the others up there climbing, hanging, zipping with the newborn driver.

Walkway forks off from the bridge, depositing us on the Riverfront Trail which takes us to the stadium, Heinz Field, south end not high at all, gear we're carrying sufficient. We send up a grappling hook and take turns hauling ourselves up the wall.

Last one up, as I join the others on the landing beside the scoreboard, a flashlight switches on. Dude sitting in a lawn chair.

"Twenty-five dollars each," he says.

"We're supposed to be meeting someone," I say.

"They're here," dude says. "That's why you gettin the group rate."

Connie Venmos the dude a hundred and we check out the open bowl of the stadium before us, dark except for rows of dim lights along the aisles. We walk around the promenade, enter a narrow alley into the stadium, and head up the steps, a body on a zipline whooshing past.

* * *

"You know," says Hellcat, sitting beside me on the top rim above the north endzone, facing out, lights of North Shore spread out below, soft rush of traffic drifting up, "being able to see so much, we got to thank Bindermaus."

"And the police in those choppers chased us off," I say.

"Funny thing about people," Hellcat says, fingernails tapping the steel beneath her, "the corruption always comes first."

"I thought the Garden of Eden came first," I say.

"Whoever tellin the story of the Garden, *thinkin* the story, came first," Hellcat says. "And if they was dreaming up paradise, innocence, couple naked frolickers—"

"They had to be coming from the other side, from corruption," I say. "Dissipation. Entropy."

Hellcat nods, looks at me. "That's why I came with my girls. First ones I found wasn't dreaming up stuff to inflate themselves, but simply ridin the currents."

I look at Hellcat, the deep lines around her mouth, the years she's carrying in her eyes.

"They couldn't have done any of this without you," I say. "None of us could have."

"Oh yes you could," she says, smile widening, lines deepening. "You may not a known what you were doing, may not a registered, but you could a done it. That horse got to run, Little Man, whether somebody whippin it or not."

I stand up, reach my arms into the night, stretching, feeling the edge of the stadium beneath my toes, turn back to the empty bowl of Heinz Field, a few scattered lights bobbing in the darkness, flashlights of girls at work, setting lines, stringing ropes.

We hear a sudden zinging of pulley on cable, and a body bursts from the darkness, lands two-footed on the walkway below us—Sheila, wearing a pink sweater and puffy white skirt.

"Oh shit, a majorette," I say, settling back down to sit on the stadium rim. "Where's your baton?"

"In your butt," she says.

Sheila steps over, leans her head against my leg, then tilts her head back, says to Hellcat, "Security guard gettin worried. Sayin he didn't realize so many were coming."

"You need money, we got a fundraiser going," I say. "Connie can set you up."

I check the GoFundMe account, up to thirteen thousand dollars, five thousand donations, mostly two or three dollars each. I click on the donation density map, the last two hours showing Pittsburgh in dark red, the map lightening to less-dense pink beyond, from Detroit down to Louisville.

"Word is out," I say, showing my phone to Hellcat, then reaching it down to Sheila.

Sheila looks, hands it back, then hands me her phone, on its screen a Tweet from Muzzy, selfie of him grinning beneath a sign says *Greyhound*, must be a bus station, caption saying, *Made it to Fort Wayne!*

"Thought we were meeting you in Pittsburgh," I text him.

"I purchased a 10-city bus pass by mistake!" he replies. "I must visit ten cities!"

Hellcat gives my shoulder a quick squeeze, scoots over, clips onto the line overhead and glides down into the darkness, her faint outline shrinking, disappearing, reappearing smaller still as she lands in the dim light of the field. Sheila reaches up for a hand, and I heave her up to sit beside me.

"So?" she says.

"Yeah," I say.

"Sure," she says.

"Yeah," I say, "sure."

"I'm glad to see you," she says. "Not glad like happy. Glad like, you know, like when you're watching the merry-go-round, and that one red horse comes around."

"Nothing special about it, just familiar," I say.

"Which horse am I?" Sheila asks.

"Don't know."

"Cause you don't think about me."

"I do."

"No you don't."

"Ok, maybe not."

"At first, I didn't get you, Little Man. Thought you were too cool, in some kind of shock or something."

"Oh yeah?"

"Then I realized it was fairness made you that way."

"I am one fair motherfucker."

"By not thinking about me, you're leaving room for everything else. So I learned not to think about you either."

"Out of fairness," I say.

Sheila turns and looks at me. "You think that means we can't love?"

I don't answer right away, not understanding. But then it comes to me, what she means by love. She means the desire to support, or be supported by, buoyed by, someone else as you lose your air and fall toward the ground.

I lean back, gaze over the side down toward the tiny lamp posts along the criss-crossing walkway, reach out and clasp Sheila's arm above the elbow.

"If we're going down, we bes grab on." I give a gentle tug and she tenses, holding her position.

Sheila stares at me a good twenty seconds, as if trying to hold me there with her eyes, like I might just disappear, like we both might, two specks out on the edge of the stadium.

Finally, she leans in and kisses me on the mouth, a firm symmetrical kiss, neither to start something nor end it, just a firm kiss that covers my mouth, anchoring the two of us to this spot for the entirety of the moment it takes to complete.

Connie texts Moses, Smiley, and me to meet down in the end zone where he shows us another batch of posts from Muzzy in Fort Wayne, standing on the lawn before the Allen County Courthouse, on the steps of the Church of the Immaculate Conception, holding a lemon-yellow parrot on his finger in the Fort Wayne Aviary, turning back from a counter holding a menu, *Lydia's Famous Lamb Chops*, two women in aprons, one on each side, pressing kisses against his cheek, Muzzy's eyes bulging with glee.

"Since I gave him the password, he's been living it up," Connie says. "Like he forgot all about Seed."

"Why not just leave him be?" Smiley says.

"Boy doesn't know where he is," I say.

"According to that Amish dude, we don't either," Smiley says.

"Only cause we're on the move," I say.

"Making sure we don't get caught up in shit," Connie says.

"Don't get raveled," says Moses.

Later, Connie tells me he bought bus tickets to Indianapolis, where we will spend the night and next day catch a bus to Fort Wayne.

10

We emerge from the bus station into the morning heat of downtown Indianapolis, and as Connie scrolls through a map looking for parks, Smiley grumbles he's tired of sleeping in trees, so we agree to get a hotel room.

Around the corner stands a sparkling gold Crowne Plaza. Not wanting to be greedy, despite the account now topping thirty thousand, the Treasurer takes Moses, only one of us who's eighteen, to check in, and the four of us pile into a room, Moses squirming for a while in the bed he shares with Smiley, moving to the floor where he squirms around some more, finally dragging a blanket down the hall to the stairwell and up to the roof. Time Connie and me get up there, Moses is dead asleep in the shade beside an exhaust fan, and it isn't long before we too are wrapped up, our bodies countering the heat by simply shutting down and drifting off, so that when Smiley joins us, grumbling about the cleaning women knocking on the door—"Housekeeping. Housekeeping. Housekeeping," he mimics—his voice blends seamlessly into our dreams of nuisances left behind.

Once daylight begins to ebb, we return to the room for showers and head out for food, passing behind a dude on a blue leather sofa in the lobby reading a tablet, dude wearing a tan fedora with a dark brown sash, looks like one of Lanny's.

Four of us grab hamburgers, wander down Indiana Avenue, till we come across a YMCA, where some tall caramel-skinned dude stops on his way in, asks Moses and Smiley if they're looking for a run.

"Damn," Smiley says, swiping the dude's hand, "didn't realize they had brothers in Indianapolis."

"This is Indiana Avenue," says the dude. "We been here since slavery."

We go inside and Caramel tells us he can only bring in two, so Connie and I pay the guest fee, sit on the side as Caramel and some other tall skinny dude make teams, Indiana brothers taking a quick lead, till Moses and Smiley realize they need to step it up, Smiley winning the game with a drive down the lane in which he elevates, fakes with the left, brings the ball back to his right, outlasting three different defenders who rise up and drop back down, releasing a finger roll over the front of the rim.

As they walk off the court, Connie and I meet Smiley with hands over our heads, but Smiley only shrugs, offers a hand at the waist.

"You killin' today," Connie says.

"Motherfucker ain't hanging *in* the air," Moses says, giving Smiley a shove, "he hanging *out* in the air."

"For a minute, felt like we were back home," Smiley says, looking at Moses.

"Lookin' 'round and shit," Connie says. "Motherfucker in the air so long, he killin time. Checkin' his phone and shit."

"Up there so long, people reportin a UFO," Moses says. "'Air Traffic Control redirectin planes and shit."

"Pilots flyin in," Connie says, pointing ahead of him, "that's a *dude* out there!"

Smiley lowers his head, walks over to get a drink of water.

"Motherfucker chillin in the ozone!" Connie calls after him. "*'Why can't nobody hang with me?'*"

Big dude, looks older than the rest, wearing jeans with white stitching and black loafers with little chains, steps over to where we're talking. Caramel sees him and steps over too.

"What up, Landscape?" Caramel says.

"Wondering what all the fuss about over here," he says.

"New York boys with some game," Connie says.

"New York boys with some mouth," Landscape says.

"That too," Connie says.

"Why you talk like you from the hood?" Landscape says. "You white as a cloud."

"You mean the cloud my boy Smiley jumping over?" Connie says, Moses covering his mouth, turning away.

"Nothing worse," Landscape says, "than a white boy tryin be black. No bigger insult."

"Nah man," Connie says, "take it the other way. You know, imitation as flattery."

"Ain't imitation, it's y'all tryin take over. We make it, you take it."

"I ain't taking nothin," Connie says. "I'm a blank canvas, and y'all spillin your colors on me."

"Shit," Landscape says.

"That's what us white boys do," Connie says, throwing me a glance. "Turn whatever color gets throwed at us. Cause we some neutral motherfuckers."

"Them police ain't neutral," Landscape says.

"I hear you," Connie says. "But that shit startin to swing back the other way."

"What, cause we got Barack and Lebron? Oprah?"

"Y'all got *language*," Connie says. "*Style.* That shit win out over the law every day. Me and my boy here, Little Man, are exhibit A. We goin your way, you ain't comin ours."

"We are some cultureless motherfuckers," I say.

Landscape looks at me and nods, offers a hand, then reaches out to Connie, then to Moses and Smiley. "Be careful," he says. "That culturelessness can lead to some nasty shit," and he strolls on back to the other side of the gym.

Back at the hotel, dude with the tan fedora's still sitting in the lobby, head down, typing into his tablet.

"Yo bro," I say, stepping in front of him, dude raising his head. "Oh shit," I say, turning back to the others. "We got us a mouse in the house!" Then back to Dr. B. "What brings you to the heartland, Binder?"

"Surely you realize," he says, "that anybody under 18 who doesn't have parental permission is considered a runaway."

"Ain't nobody runnin."

"Because you're going from state to state, we had to contact the FBI. They're rounding up kids in Louisville right now, the ones whose parents have filed reports."

"Everybody here is cool."

"Not Smiley," says Dr. B. "His mother wants him home."

"What are you, some kind of bounty hunter?"

"I represent the New York City School Board," he says.

"This ain't about school."

Bindermaus stands. "It's always about school," he says.

I walk over to the boys waiting by the elevator.

"Your mom wants you home," I say to Smiley.

"She been texting me," he says.

"They're saying we have to have parental permission."

"Dr. B gon take me?" Smiley says, looking over at Bindermaus.

"What you need to do anyway," Moses says. "Way you been worryin."

We go back up to the room where Smiley packs up, leaving his climbing gear on the floor, and return to Bindermaus in the lobby.

"Let me grab somethin eat," Smiley says, and he walks over to the snack stand, selects about ten candy bars, signs for them.

Stashing the candy in his pack, Smiley trudges back to us, looks from me to Connie to Moses.

"Guess I'll see you guys," he says.

"Take care of your mom," Moses says. "We'll be out there when you're ready."

-

11

We split up Smiley's gear, board an early morning Greyhound which chugs across the flat Indiana farmland through the summer haze. After Muncie, traffic thins, an occasional silo or water tower rising up from the countryside, emblazoned with a town name, Van Buren, Plum Tree, Zanesville. Otherwise, just people in cars and pickups crawling along the flat earth.

I doze off to sleep, wake to a shake from Moses as we enter downtown Fort Wayne.

"This is one big-ass fort," I say.

"Out here in the middle of nowhere," Connie says.

"Guess what else in the middle of nowhere?" Moses says. "Name a city, any city."

"Not New York," Connie says.

"Cause you lived there don't make it somewhere," Moses says.

"It's not about how big it is," I say. "It's about what's around it."

"Then this whole planet is in the middle of nowhere," Connie says.

"Bingo," I say.

We get off the bus and Connie texts Muzzy, going back and forth a few minutes, then orders an Uber and slides the phone in a pocket.

"Started telling me about some Burmese mosque he goes to," Connie says, "sayin how friendly everybody is. So I said, 'Oh yeah? What mosque? I'll check it out online,' and he gave up the name."

We pull in the circular drive before a mustard-colored stucco building with some kind of dark woodwork—fig tree? walnut?—walk through an archway up a path to the main entrance.

Inside, we check out a large prayer room on one side, couple smaller rooms on the other side, all empty, floors covered in Persian rugs.

"Long as we here waiting," Moses says, and he leads the way into the larger room, where he drops to his knees, raises his hands above his head, and bows down, Connie and me doing the same.

"What we praying for?" Connie asks.

"Up to you," Moses says.

"Suppose he wants to pray to Jesus?" I say. "Or to some Hindu god, Shiva or somebody?"

"Or how about I ain't prayin to nobody, just prayin *for* somethin," Connie says. "Like money, or to get laid? Or to spite some motherfucker?"

"That what you *supposed* to pray for," Moses says. "Pleasure and power."

"Nah man," Connie says, "there's principles. In all the religions. Helping the downtrodden, shit like that."

"You can *say* that's what it's about," Moses says, "but soon as people start practicing the shit, them principles change pretty fast. Now bow your heads and pray to whatever God you got the best chance with."

"Yes sir, Moses Imam," Connie says.

"Dear God," Moses begins.

"Dear Everything," I say.

"Dear Nothing," says Connie.

"Dear Whoever," Moses says, "please grant us health and prosperity. So that we may outlive our enemies."

"That's not so bad," Connie says.

"So that we can get a leg up on the competition and take the biggest piece of cake," Moses continues.

"Biggest piece of ass," Connie says.

"Ooooh," I chime in.

Moses bows down and kisses the ground between his hands, moans some kind of gibberish chant, then continues his prayer. "We offer you our hearts, our souls, our minds—"

"Everything but our wallets," Connie says.

"And definitely not our GoFundMe account," I say. "Please Everything, do not fuck with our cash flow."

"—we offer you our love and eternal atonement for our sins. And if possible—" Moses glances back at Connie and me— "because we are unable to make it regularly to church—"

"Or Mosque," Connie says.

"Or Everywhere," I say.

"Or Target," says Connie. "Or Dick's."

"—If possible," Moses continues, "please accept this one prayer for all of our sins, past and future."

"Because we ain't ever goin be praying again," Connie says.

"Because we are nothing but pagan—" I say.

"Please accept this one-time prayer," Moses says.

"Prayers ain't ever answered after one time," Connie says.

"Cause that's how He gets you hooked," Moses says. "Not by answering your prayers but by *not* answering em, making you come back even harder."

"Don't make sense," Connie says.

"Sure it does," I say. "Keep having your faith rejected, motherfuckers gonna double down, find some other shit they got to do better."

"Cause we always fuckin up somewhere," Moses says.

"Yo," Connie says, and we turn and see a man in a white robe and fat white headband standing in the doorway.

"You must be Ahmed's friends," dude says, stepping into the room. "He told me about you. I am Imam Rashid."

"Is Ahmed here?" I ask.

"He will come for The Asr Prayer, today at 4:24."

"Not the same time every day?" I ask.

"What are you, writing a book?" Connie says to me.

"Just saying, why 4:24?"

"The Asr begins when the shadow is twice as long as the body," the imam says.

"You from Tunisia?" Moses asks.

"I am Rohingya, from Myanmar."

"Twice as long?" Connie says. He stands up, looks down at his shadow. "Mine ain't even once as long."

"Outside, dumb ass, once the sun starts droppin," Moses says.

"Here is Ahmed," the imam says, and exits the room.

We follow into the foyer, where we see through a window Muzzy locking his bike to the filigreed iron railing. He enters the foyer, sees us, and stops dead in his tracks, breaking into a broad smile but not moving forward. The imam slips off to another room.

We walk over, tell Muzzy not to worry, we're just here to check him out, see if he still wants to go find Seed.

"Seed," he says. "Yes, of course."

"We fixin to get back on that trail tonight," Moses says.

"Yes, yes," Muzzy says. "I have prayer now and I have to help my landlady move some things. And then I will text you."

We shake his hand and are halfway down the walkway when the imam calls to us from a side door, stepping out onto the lawn, glancing back over his shoulder.

"Ahmed needs to go with you," the imam says in a loud whisper.

"Why's that?" I ask.

"He eats too much."

"Say what?" Moses says.

The imam continues over to us. "Our women bake things every day for afternoon snack after Asr, and—" he breaks off, exhaling, shaking his head. "Ahmed is a good young man. But Ms. Sakira says that after eating too many of the snacks, each night he is coming in the house with a bag of Big Macs and French fries. And now he is using those apps to have food delivered here. He needs to go with you."

"Now?" Moses says.

"I will help."

The imam leads us back into the prayer room, about twenty people having gathered, leans down and whispers something to Muzzy. Muzzy looks at him like a child who's been told it's time to go home, slowly stands and follows the imam out.

In the foyer, Muzzy says goodbye to the imam, kisses him on both cheeks.

"Please tell Ms. Sakira I will pick up my things now and will not see her after prayer," he says. Then to us, "There is a MacDonald's near the house for dinner."

"We ain't stopping," Moses says.

We step down off the porch, walk toward the street, another Uber Connie ordered already there.

"Ahmed!" the Imam calls from the front porch.

The five of us stop and turn back.

Imam Rashid points a straight-armed finger at Muzzy. "No Grubhub!"

12

We continue west into Illinois, moving slower over farmland in the Greyhound than we did humping through the city, covering more mileage yet at the same time, with so much ground to cover, hardly moving. Funny how the more ground you cover, the slower you move. Reminds me how as a kid, when we'd head out at nighttime, how fast we seemed to run. Cause we couldn't see anything. Daylight is a bitch; slows you down, gives you more to think about, worry about. No wonder everybody's filling in the space, with buildings, schools, traffic lights. Trying to get a handle on eternity, get some purchase.

I drift off, slinking into the empty seat at my side, rouse in the late afternoon as we cross the Illinois River, passing through a steel cage.

"This bridge like the Fort Duquesne," Connie says, one row up.

"And that Outerbridge," Moses says from across the aisle.

"They're all cantilevered," I say.

Connie and Moses look at me, then at each other.

"Home boy do love his books," Connie says.

I hold up my phone. "It's all right here," I say. "Everything you need to know."

"Everything you *don't* need to know," Moses says.

We slide off the bridge, take an exit into downtown Peoria.

"This a city too," Moses says.

"Got to put them Urban Outfitters somewhere," Connie says.

"Churches, Home Depots, Urban Outfitters," I say.

"My grandpappy always sayin," Moses says, "every time anybody want try something new, 'How that gon play in Peoria?' I always figure Peoria some one-horse Podunk."

"Definitely got more than one horse," Connie says.

With an hour to kill before the transfer, the four of us load on our packs, wander back along the gridded streets toward the river and wind our way north, passing a docked riverboat with a huge red paddle-wheel, come upon the steel cantilevered bridge we just crossed, pass beneath the Interstate, up onto a path into Riverfront Park, and stop at three granite boulders etched with song lyrics by some dude called Dan Fogelberg, couple of women in woven summer hats standing by holding tissues.

We read the engravings.

"Dude was deep," Connie says.

"Reminds me of Echebbi," says Muzzy. "Tunisian poet."

One of the women overhears us. "Dan was the heart and soul of Illinois," she says.

The other woman wipes her eyes. "Every summer," she says, "we come for the fair and to see the memorial."

"The Heart of Illinois Fair," says the first. "Not what it used to be, but we wouldn't miss it."

We continue up the path, Connie YouTubing Dan Fogelberg, playing his song, "Illinois," at full phone volume.

Third time through, four of us are walking up the riverfront path singing along with the refrain, walking toward another steel-cage cantilevered bridge, under another overpass, and into the thick tree-cover of Grandview Park.

> And it looks like you're gonna
> Have to see me again
> And it looks like you're gonna
> Have to see me again
> Illinois, oh Illinois
> I'm your boy.

"Kids been posting from a forest preserve up ahead," Connie says.

We turn onto a winding road, make our way north along the shoulder.

"Grandview Drive," Connie says, looking up from his phone. "According to Teddy Roosevelt, most beautiful road in America."

"Who was Teddy Roosevelt?" Muzzy asks.

"Went by FDR," Connie answers. "Got shot from some book suppository in Cuba."

"That's some raveled history you talkin," Moses says.

"All you need to know," Connie says, tapping his phone.

We wind our way around a couple more curves, occasional car passing, come to a sign for a trailhead, turn into the deep shade of Peoria Forest Park.

"A forest surrounded by city," Connie says.

"And the city surrounded by forest," Muzzy says.

"By forest, he mean nature," Moses says.

"Everything is surrounded by nature," Muzzy says. "Echebbi said it is the one thing we can never escape. Even in death."

"That's why we call it the Heartland," Moses says, and the four of us sing another round of the chorus:

And it looks like you're gonna
Have to see me again
And it looks like you're gonna
Have to see me again
Illinois, oh Illinois
I'm your boy

Deeper into the forest, we walk beneath a colony of treehouses made from cardboard and sheets, Connie calling up, a couple of sleepy faces poking out, rest of us following the lyrics on our screens, song playing again from the beginning.

Dusty day dawning
Three hours late
Open the curtains
And let the rest wait.

"Who's coming to the fair?" Connie calls up.

My mind goes running
Three thousand miles east
I may miss the harvest
But I won't miss the feast.

A couple of kids emerge from their makeshift abodes, sling down on ropes, and we continue on, singing the chorus, more fog-eyed dudes descending from the leaves, joining the chorus as we march from the woods back into the city.

Muzzy steps up beside me. "We are going to miss the transfer," he says.

"This America, dude," I tell him. "Got plenty more busses—probably more than we got people."

Line of stragglers stretching into the distance behind, we pass under a highway, continue onto a sidewalk along a four-lane road.

South California
Your sun is too cold
It looks like your hills
Have been raped of their gold.
I should have come out
When I was first told
This lamb has got to
Return to the fold.

Then the chorus, booming now, more voices joining:

And it looks like you're gonna
Have to see me again
And it looks like you're gonna
Have to see me again...

Connie leads us beneath the entry banner into Expo Gardens, past a pen with hogs, a spinning Ferris wheel with nobody on it, a line of patronless game booths, only a pair of dads in cowboy hats loitering nearby with their kids.

"Where is everyone?" I ask one, his left eye squinting half closed.

"Over to the mall, I 'spect," he says.

"Or sittin home on their devices," says the other dad.

"Albert," first dad says, seeing the throng of kids coming up behind us, "they must a closed the mall."

We lead the mob past a Budweiser truck, hear the humming vibrato of electric guitars, and follow a sign pointing toward the Grandstand, see the near-empty bleachers first, then the stage, a denim-clad chick taking a bow, rest of the band bowing in turn, a few clapping people sitting in the stands.

The four of us climb onto the stage as the band departs, the rest of our parade, must be up to a few hundred, filing into the rows of seats.

Moses steps up to the mic for the lead singer, Muzzy, Connie, and me moving to the mics for the other band members.

"Good evening, Peoria!" Moses shouts, stands half full, more kids streaming in, flood lamps mounted to poles blinking on as the daylight fades.

"How we feeling?" Moses shouts, crowd responding with a half-hearted murmur, kids still taking seats.

"Illinois," Moses bellows, "*how we feeling*?" And this time the crowd responds with a roar.

"Feels good to be home," Moses says, glancing at me and the boys, who nod in agreement. "Like we didn't even know we were away," he says, "till we got home."

The crowd of kids, nearly all boys, a few girls mixed in, begin to chant, "Peoria! Peoria! Peoria!"

"And they say this fair lost its mojo!" Moses calls.

"Hello, Peoria!" Muzzy shouts into his mic, and the crowd roars.

"We may never leave!" Moses calls.

"How's *this* gonna play in Peoria?" I shout into my mic.

Moses raises a hand in the air, conductor style, and when he brings it down, the four of us begin, reading from our phones, Connie and Muzzy pushing each note hard, Moses and me low-keying it, providing what turns out to be something like harmony.

> Dusty day dawning
> Three hours late

Open the curtains
And let the rest wait…

By the third verse, a lot of the crowd has pulled up the lyrics and begun to sing along, others switching on and raising their flashlights, rocking back and forth.

Flat on the prairies
Soil and stone
Stretching forever
Taking me home
'Cause I've got a woman
Who waits for me there
And I need a breath of that
Sweet country air.

"Everybody!" Moses cries out, and the voices of the nearly full stadium swell into crescendo:

And it looks like you're gonna
Have to see me again!
And it looks like you're gonna
Have to see me again!
And it looks like you're gonna
Have to see me again!
Illinois, oh Illinois!
Illinois, I'm your boy!

Moses waggles his mic from the stand and holds it straight out before him, rest of us following suit, and together we release them, microphones clattering onto the stage's wooden flooring.

13

On our way to catch the ten o'clock bus, we stop at a 7/11, and once we're seated on the bus, Moses doles out chicken salad sandwiches sealed in triangle containers.

"Find one of these motherfuckers anytime, anyplace," he says.

"Blue dots floating in ether," I say, stretching my head back against the headrest. "Not so bad."

"Not at all," Moses concurs, pressing the armrest button, reclining the maximum four inches.

"One minute ago," Muzzy says, "you were talking about being home. Like I was feeling in Fort Wayne. Now you are saying you are floating blue dots."

"Cause we knew we weren't stayin," Moses says.

"Only way to truly be somewhere," I say.

Muzzy looks from me back to Moses. "*'Kunt 'aela 'anah kan hban li'anah eindama ghadar, ghadir 'iilaa al'abad,*" he says. "I knew it was love," he says, translating, choosing each word carefully, "because when it left, it left forever."

"Echebbi?" Connie says.

Muzzy nods.

"Nah man," Moses says, "that some Fogelberg."

"Fogleberg sang about returning," Muzzy says. "Echebbi is saying he must leave."

Moses shrugs, pushes out his lower lip. "Same thing."

"A body's got to leave one place," Connie says, "if it's gonna return to another."

I stand up, walk ahead a few rows and stand in the aisle. "Connie, come here," I say.

Connie rises and approaches.

"Don't leave!" Moses calls out, clutching at Connie's waist.

"He's not leaving you," I say. "He's coming to talk to me."

Connie gives me a hand swipe, turns back toward his seat.

"Thought you were leaving for good," Moses says.

"I was," says Connie. "I did."

As we eat, passengers trickle onto the bus, each of us protecting the seats at our side, except for Connie, asleep against the window, an old dude in plaid jacket settling in beside him.

"How's that gon play in Peoria?" Moses mutters to no one, shaking his head, biting into his sandwich.

"It is true," Muzzy says from behind me, "that for a place to be somewhere, it must be in the middle of nowhere."

"Ahh," says Moses, "the pupil is becoming the master."

"Except for one place," says the man in plaid beside Connie, raising a finger out where we can see it.

"Where's that?" I ask.

"Center Point, Iowa."

"That's where we're going," Moses says.

"Next stop after Cedar Rapids," says Connie, rousing.

"You can say it's a stop," says the man in plaid. "But Center Point is not a place. Not a location."

The bus lurches forward, ambles ahead to a stoplight, and chugs up the ramp onto the highway.

"Where I'm from and where I'm going," muses the man. "A place that is no place."

Muzzy moves up to the empty seat across the aisle from the man in plaid.

"We are going to find our friend," Muzzy says to him.

"That you should be able to do."

"And we will take him with us," Muzzy says.

"Now *that* may prove difficult. Center Point is the heart of the heartland, the center not merely of the state of Iowa but, in a manner of speaking, of the entire United States, a place at the mercy of powerful centripetal forces, not a widening gyre as the poet said, but a *collapsing* gyre, the center falling into the center, tumbling into itself, collapsing into a single molecular point."

"Sounds like a black hole," I say.

The man in plaid pauses, glancing from Muzzy to Connie, then to me and Moses.

"Where you boys from?" he asks.

"New York," Moses says.

"And you're going to find a friend?"

"Yes," says Muzzy, "Seed."

"You're traveling across the country, from the Big Apple, the shining queen of the somewheres into the black hole of the world." He holds his eyes on Muzzy, who shifts in his seat. "In order to unplant a seed."

"Unravel him," Moses says.

"Yes," says the man in plaid, "agents of the unraveling—" he releases a sigh—"I remember hearing you'd be coming."

We slumber through the heartland, stopping at Cedar Rapids and continuing on, Moses in his ear buds gazing out at the slow-passing farmland, till finally the bus pulls onto the exit ramp for Center Point.

"Where are you going now?" Muzzy asks the man in plaid, brakes hissing as we enter the station.

The man glances back, then leans across the aisle, gripping Muzzy's arm with long bony fingers. "First, I'm going to cash my gov'ment check for two hundred sixty-five dollars," he says. "Then I will meet my concubine of twenty-seven years in an air-conditioned room on the top floor of the Econolodge where we will open wide the curtains and see what happens next."

14

Bus unloads at dusk and Connie, face in his phone, says to follow him, Seed's house is a mile away. We hump up Main Street, pass a church with a few kids on the lawn in sleeping bags, couple of them lifting their heads to watch us. Streetlights above blinking on, we cut the corner of Wakema Park and see more camped out, then pass a larger park with two back-to-back baseball fields dotted with kids in sleeping bags, couple of pup tents.

"Check it out," Moses says, looking over his shoulder, kids behind hoisting backpacks over shoulders, rolling up sleeping bags, trailing along.

Connie leads us out from beneath the last of the streetlights, farmland opening out on one side beneath a darkening purple sky, on the other side, the jagged outline of brush that conceals a creek, which when the street curves close we hear crickling.

Connie stops beside a radio tower, upper half visible against the sky, and ahead I see a house with a couple of softly-lit windows, beside it the dark shape of a storage shed or barn.

"Seed home?" I ask Muzzy.

"He is not answering," Muzzy says.

The four of us walk up the front steps and knock on the door, the growing group of followers halting on the street.

Door opens, revealing a tired-looking dude with a short gray buzzcut. "Can I help you boys?"

"We're looking for Seed," I say.

"For *what?*"

"Bobby," Muzzy says.

Dude turns back, calls into the house, "Bobby! I believe your entourage has arrived!" And he drifts back into the house.

Seed steps out onto the porch, quietly swipes each of our hands.

"I told you we were coming," Muzzy says. "Why did you stop texting?"

"Cops raided our platform, found a bag of weed, so my dad took my phone."

"We just passed the tower," Moses says.

"There's two platforms," Seed says. "The Salon halfway up and Penthouse on top." Seed takes a look back into the house. "Give me twenty minutes," he says, "I'll meet you in The Salon."

Seed starts to go in, then turns back, stands still peering past us. I turn to see what's got his attention. Sprinkled amongst the settling darkness, dark figures, every fourth or fifth one topped with a faintly glowing oblong, a hoody-shrouded face illuminated by a phone, figures receding into the distance like the *farolitos* Lanny and his neighbors used to set out on the fire escapes at Christmas.

The Salon has seat cushions and pillows, and a plastic tarp for a ceiling with a pull-cord that rolls back to reveal the stars.

One way, we can see the lights of the town; the other way, nothing but thick brewing darkness.

Seed tells us his parents let him quit school to work with his dad and uncle making fertilizer, that he's saving to buy a pickup.

"Can't go anywhere without wheels," he says.

"The imam in Fort Wayne has a Dodge Ram," Muzzy says. "420 horsepower and 600 pounds of torque."

"Who you hanging with?" Connie asks Seed.

"Couple dudes still in school come chill in The Salon. But they won't go any higher."

"Shit," Moses says. "You'd think out here motherfuckers tryin rise up high as they can."

"Nah," Seed says. "Here in the mid-west, people hunker down."

"In Fort Wayne," Muzzy says, "the people were all very nice."

Moses stares at Muzzy. "What kind of Kool-Aid they give you?" he says.

"We're going to keep moving west if you want to come," I say to Seed.

"I don't know," Seed says.

Connie leans over, whispers in my ear he has an idea. I tell Moses and Muzzy to sit tight with Seed, Connie and I will be right back.

Connie swings a leg over the railing, and I follow down between the bodies perching on cross bars, couple of them asking about Seed, if he's okay, if he'll be coming with us, Connie telling them sure, we just need to figure some shit out.

We jump to the ground and head back to Seed's house, Seed's father again answering the door.

"Got a second?" Connie says.

"Long as you're not looking for money," Seed's dad says, letting us in, the three of us sitting before a large television screen with four people in boxes arguing.

"We need you to tell Seed it's okay," Connie says.

"What is?"

"Him coming with us."

"Where you going?"

"West," I say. "Summer trip we started back in New York."

"Some kind of education program?" Seed's dad asks.

"Sure," I say. I slide up to the edge of the cushion and lean forward, "Only not *in* school, *out* of it."

Seed's dad sits there a moment, taking my measure.

"School's a fucking joke," he says.

"You got that right," Connie says.

Seed's mother appears in the rear in a wheelchair, blanket over legs. Recovery must not have gone too well. Connie stands and so do I.

"Boys want Seed to join em on their summer tour," Seed's dad tells her. "These two come from New York."

She wheels over, extends a hand to each of us. "I never wanted him to come back to Iowa," she says.

"We realize Seed's been working with you," I say to his dad, "and may be unsure about leaving."

"There's no way he'll go unless he knows you'll be okay without him," Connie says.

The old man peers at Connie a moment, then at me. "You come all the way from New York City?"

"Yes sir," I say.

"All that way to Center Point?"

"Let me show you something," I say.

Mom sits tight, and the three of us walk out onto the porch and look out at the tower, its silhouette lumpy with bodies before the faint glow from town.

"Those are kids," Connie says. "All come to get Seed."

* * *

Climbing back up the tower, the bodies move apart to allow our passage, first Connie pulling himself onto the platform, then me, then Seed's dad, who straightens and looks toward the lights of the town, then steps across to the other side and peers into the darkness.

"Which way can you see farther?" he asks.

"If you looking for something particular," Moses says, "look toward the light. If you looking for something else, something you ain't seen before, look the other way."

"There's our house," Seed's father says, "right there between. Town on one side, nothing at all on the other."

Seed's father turns and looks at Moses. "What about now?" he asks. "What am I seeing now?"

Moses doesn't answer, just lets the man's eyes soak up all they can from his own dark, lightly shimmering face.

"You come all the way from New York to get my boy?" the old man says to him.

"Yes," Moses says.

The old man rolls in his lips, nods, steps over to Seed. He reaches into his back pocket, takes out his wallet, removes a sheaf of bills.

I place my hand on the old man's. "Keep it," I say. "We got money coming in from all over the country."

Seed's dad replaces the wallet, reaches into a different pocket, removes Seed's phone, hands it to him.

"Guess I knew when we moved here to the outskirts, I was giving you a choice," he says.

Seed's dad steps to the edge of the platform, turns back to Seed, slides his feet apart, widening his base, bends his knees and lowers his hands between them, fingers interlocked to make a stirrup.

"I'm ready," he says.

I hand Seed Smiley's harness, and he wiggles into it, clips onto a line above, and with two quick steps plants a foot in his dad's locked fingers, whereupon his father, with a loud grunt, propels him up and out into the night.

BOOK TWO

15

Motherfuckers getting after it tonight, Seed saying the Cedar River's a mile ahead, Connie sliding that finger across his phone to confirm, Seed taking off like a wild horse slipped the lasso, rest of us trying to keep up, dudes behind trailing along, some splintering off onto different routes, seeking unoccupied places to sleep, Walmarts or small town mom and pops to restock at.

Almost to the river, the farmland ends and we enter thick forest which, our local tour guide, Seed, explains, is on both sides of the river, recreation areas where Iowans hike and picnic, and up into the trees we go, using our phone lights to string lines, connect ropes, our thinned-down herd—no, what do you call a group of monkeys, a tribe? A platoon?

No, a troop. We are one big motherfucking troop and we are tearing through these Iowa trees, heading west, then north-west, leap-frogging, rope-swinging, Seed leading the way, his hands and feet barely touching the branches.

Each night we wind along the Cedar River till we find a place with strong branches and openings for activity, one night the four of us riding a zip line back to check out a group of dudes trailing along—from just outside Pittsburgh, one of them tells us—doing some kind of free-fall stunt, where one climbs up to the highest branch that'll hold him, finds a clear shaft down and dives head first, others spread out below, the challenge for them to gather quicker than the dude can fall.

We watch different kids take turns ascending, disappearing into the thin branches, someone up there directing them to particular spots, branches and leaves rustling, dudes below peering up, till the jumper jumps and they converge, assembling themselves into a three-tier human net, the falling body entering the top level of arms at rocket speed but slowing through each layer, emerging on its feet, the human net disassembling, kids separating in silence to listen for the next jumper.

Finally, the last person, the one directing, lets out a cry and drops, kids on the ground barely assembling in time to catch him.

My boys and me hop a line down and see that last jumper is the driver from Pittsburgh.

"Told you this boy had skill," Moses says.

"Think it was Smiley said that," I say.

"Smiley," Moses says, shaking his head.

"All about letting go," driver says.

"Trusting that your brothers will catch you," Muzzy says.

"Not really," driver says.

"Dude movin on from that," I say.

"But they do catch you," Muzzy says. "Every time."

"Every time *so far*," driver says.

In the morning we crash, in the afternoon resuming our journey north-west, following the tree-lined river till we reach a wood-plank bridge, cross over to the western bank, staying left at each fork we come to, Connie announcing the names of the waterways, Buffalo Creek, Otter Creek . . .

Four or five days in, the creeks peter out, and we take to the fields, Iowa kids in towns ahead posting addresses of unlocked barns, silos, sometimes laying out tarps for us beneath the stars, some joining us, others not quite ready, that GoFundMe balance continuing to grow.

Couple times, a farmer or county sheriff stops us, then seeing the numbers of kids coming across the fields to our rear, politely asks what this is about. We show them the Twitter account, *From Sea to Shining Sea: Unseeding America*, tell them it's a summer adventure program led by New York City Science Teacher, Consuela Erebus, Sheriff in Sioux City saying yeah he saw something on the news, let him know if we need anything.

Outside Sioux City, we follow the Missouri River to the Lewis and Clark Marina and when Muzzy says it'd be cool to ride a boat along the river, I turn to Connie who says the account is now north of two hundred grand, then to Moses who says, "Why the fuck not?" and we enter the rental office, Moses pulling the marina operator into conversation, dude telling how his great grandfather was a homesteader, given a claim and a hundred dollars from Teddy Roosevelt, Muzzy whispering to me, "That's the guy who was shot in the library," Moses telling the dude his people were *reverse* homesteaders, leaving the farms for the cities, Moses' people very possibly moving into the same apartment the marina dude's granddad vacated, the dude giving Moses a homie shake, offering us a sweet 22-foot twin-engine Seacrest II, Moses slapping his back pockets with both hands, saying Shit, he forgot his mariner's license, dude saying hold on, stepping into the back room, returning with his brother whom he says has nothing to do anyway.

Hour or so in, Captain Bro-Bro says we can only go as far north as the Gavins Point Dam, so when we see an enormous cement wall running one shore to the other, jets of water shooting out, dude pulls the boat to the South Dakota side and we strip down to boxers, stuff sneakers and pants in backpacks, wade in through thigh-deep water.

Onshore, Connie checks his phone. "Welcome to the Chief White Crane Recreation Area," he says.

We pull on our clothes, a treeless neighborhood on one side, thick-treed woodlands on the other, head for the shade of trees, gathering up dead branches, tying off a couple platforms, filling in the uneven creases with leaves, and settle in for a good sleep.

I wake in the early morning light to quivering, ululating voices in the woods.

"Some dudes from the Yankton Rez," Connie, lying beside me, says. "Offered to take us out on the reservoir. Up here!" he calls.

"We some seafarin motherfuckers," Moses says, hammocked up to the side, voice husky with sleep. "Now that we in the middle of the continent."

We pack up our gear and two dudes, Tommy and Hotah, wearing cargo shorts and Denver Nuggets jerseys, lead us to a pickup truck, our posse of five climbing in back.

Isn't long before the truck pulls off the roadway toward the river, passing a sign, *Welcome to the Lewis and Clark Recreation Area*, Tommy flashing a card to the guy at the booth, Hotah calling back through the passenger window, "Indians get in free!"

Truck parks in a spot before the marina, a basketball court to the side, some old dude out there with a black pony tail, dressed in jeans and cowboy boots, shooting long set shots. Tommy and Hotah walk over to the court, five of us following, another truckload of kids continuing past to the marina.

"Three on three," Tommy says. "We'll take the old guy."

"Long as he don't step on my foot with them boots," Moses says, the guy ignoring him, busy setting up and shooting, after each miss walking intently after the wayward ball.

"Okay, Hoss," Tommy says, "let's show these New Yorkers how the game is played."

The man smiles, shoots another long set shot, this time Hotah collecting the rebound and moving out to the key.

"Game to seven," Hotah says.

Muzzy and I sit on the side, letting Connie and Seed play with Moses, who quickly scores the first basket, then the second.

The old guy hardly moves, hanging out beyond the 3-point line to hoist up set shots when they give him the ball, which surprisingly, Tommy and Hotah, who both have some skill, do on every possession.

"Damn," Moses says, ending the game 7-0, "y'all passin the ball too much."

"We play different than you guys," Tommy says.

"White boys play different than them too," Connie says. "Brothers do that individual, playground shit. White boys more organized, like a army."

"Take this guy," Tommy says, watching the old guy raise the ball above his head, set himself, and send it toward the rim. "All he wants to do is solve the puzzle of how to make that ball go through the hoop. You black guys play with zest. Every move an opportunity to show the world something new."

"Gotta do it where we can," Moses says.

"We Indians gave up on that a long time ago," Tommy says.

For a while, we all stand around rebounding for the old dude who moves from one spot to another, shooting his set shots, every now and then one going in, at which point he pauses with furrowed brow, reflecting on his method, trying with his next shot to duplicate it, but unable to.

The other group long gone, Tommy and Hotah take us to the marina and the seven of us pile into a small outboard motorboat and head out onto the lake.

"Once upon a time," Moses says, "y'all must a had this whole thing to yourselves."

"Wasn't nothing but a river back in the day," Tommy says. "Later on was when they built the damn and made this reservoir."

"They got a visitor center on the Nebraska side," Hotah says, "tell you everything you need to know."

"Everything you don't need to know," says Tommy, Connie turning back to me with a look, like where did he get that from?

"Let's take em," Hotah says.

"Okay," says Tommy, removing a couple of small tools from a side compartment, "but we gotta go Indian style."

Tommy and Hotah lead us from the truck past the main building, to the back side of a restroom facility, which has a section missing a chunk of beige bricks, the hole reaching through to the sheetrock inside. Tommy removes a chisel and small hammer from his pocket and after about seven or eight taps has a brick in his hand, then, after a few more taps, a second one.

"My dad and me are fixing up the back yard," he says. "We finished the wood-fired oven and started a patio."

"Must be taking a while," Connie says.

"Indians ain't in no hurry," Hotah says.

They got this huge cast-metal statue of Sacagawea out on the lawn, which I've wandered over to check out, wondering how they cast a statue so large, looking for a seam, figuring they must have put it together in pieces.

"One big-ass apology," a voice says at my shoulder, Sheila's voice. "What the fuck you doing at a visitor center, Little Man?" she says.

"Trying to figure out how they made this big Indian chick."

Tommy's voice pipes up from my other shoulder. "You think she's big?" he says. "We need to take you to Crazy Horse."

Sheila checks her phone, flips and scrolls for a second. "Look like we headin the same way. See you boys in the Black Hills."

Sheila winks at me, runs off, and I walk with Tommy and Hotah, each with a brick in hand, to the chain-link fence at the edge of the property where, standing high above the river, we see a large herd of women on the shore with backpacks, a few stragglers joining, group beginning to move up the shore, front ones first, few seconds later back ones, entire group stretching thin, then swelling out into the widening strand.

16

Sun sets and full moon pokes its face up in the east as we begin climbing to Black Elk Peak, the five of us, plus Tommy and Hotah, who grew up in the Black Hills and know a short cut, scrabbling up, up, settling down on a flat shelf beside the jagged granite peak, dark figures trailing after us in the moonlight.

Couple bars of coverage, I scroll through posts showing kids camping in Pine Ridge Rez, Badlands National Park, Custer Park, one from Sheila of women gathering in the hills behind Rushmore, Black Elk Peak situated halfway between them and Crazy Horse, giving us a good vantage point as bodies continue settling in.

"Might be time for a speech," I say to Moses.

Moses shrugs, lifts himself up, steps up onto a granite boulder at his side, his dark figure looming before the plum-gray sky.

"Yo!" he calls out.

"What up, dude?" returns one voice, followed by another, "Yo, cuz!"

"It's hot shit seeing y'all up on this mountain!" Moses calls.

"Hot shit seeing you!" returns a voice, and Moses jumps down from the boulder.

"Is that it?" someone calls.

"Is that what?" Moses answers.

"Alright," says the voice, "we hear you," and a soft wave of applause ripples down the mountain.

"What about you, Little Man?" somebody calls, and I step up onto the boulder.

"It's hot shit seeing you all tonight!" I call down the mountain.

"Hot shit seeing you, Little Man!" several voices call back.

As I'm stepping down, somebody calls, "Is that it?"

"Is that what?" I answer, jumping to the ground, another round of light applause rippling away.

Hotah leads us through the dim light from the moon, now at forty-five degrees, down a trail, back up over a mountain and on around the next, kids sprinkled across the landscape, mostly chilling in small groups, some working with flashlights on the peaks installing zip lines from crag to crag, pounding pitons into granite. We follow Hotah around a huge dome, can barely make out Crazy Horse's carved face in the distance and a crowd of people down below.

"Dude must a been bad-ass," Moses says.

We proceed to the edge of the crowd, Hotah explaining these meetings have been happening for months, three groups debating, one that includes the family that owns the site, arguing they need time to complete the sculpture, Crazy Horse's extended arm and horse barely started, their progress dependent on tourist revenue; a second group, which claims to include descendants of Crazy Horse (Hotah saying he'd like to see their 23andMe charts), who say the memorial is a defilement of their sacred grounds; and a third group, a mix of Indians and white people, arguing that the monument is fine but ownership needs to be returned to the Oglala Sioux.

A white woman in bandanna steps onto a wooden platform.

"This is not a monument but a memorial!" she shouts. "We aren't building it to make ourselves feel better, throwing you Indians a bone—not like they're glorifying those four men over on Rushmore. This is a memorial, an expression of grief we can all join in together!"

"You're making quite a profit off that expression!" someone shouts.

"On Indian land!" shouts another.

"*Stolen* Indian land!" calls a third.

"Shit is thick," Moses grumbles.

"Let's check out the girls, uh, women, over on Rushmore," Connie says.

"Shit's even thicker over there," says Tommy, "y'all trying to pay us off."

"In 1980," says Tommy, "you offered us 17 million to surrender the land, our sacred land, our . . ." he trails off, looking to Muzzy for the word.

"Mecca," I say.

"Makkah," says Muzzy.

"*After* you built those four heads? No way," Hotah says. "Ain't takin no blood money."

"What's the quickest way there?" Connie asks.

"Quickest way will still take a while," Hotah says.

"Lines they're settin up might help," I say.

Following a path up between the granite crags, we come upon a group of dudes, moon higher, light stronger, riveting a cable, looping it over a spire, and sending off a body. I'm about to ask how they got that long a length of low-gauge cable up so high, then hear an engine rev and see an ATV rumble off over the rocks.

We strap on our harnesses and one-at-a-time zip two hundred yards or so to the next crag.

In less than an hour, we're back at Black Elk Peak where we chill a while in the moonlight.

"Every spring we would travel to Makkah," Muzzy says, leaning back against a boulder. "On the way, my parents would take me camping in the desert. We would cook dinner and lie down beneath the stars, until suddenly one would speed across the sky, and my father would say, 'Are you listening, Ahmed? Are you listening to Allah?'"

"You miss your folks?" Moses says.

"I do," Muzzy says. "But also I don't."

"How bout you?" Moses says to Connie, sitting on a rock.

"Nothing to miss," Connie says. "My dad only came around when he needed something. And my mom, well she tried, but I don't know, it was like she tried too hard."

"What about you?" I say to Moses. "What about our clear-eyed prophet? What you leaving behind?"

"My mom was all set to move out of New York, only one in her family, when she got pregnant with me," Moses says, leaning back, both elbows on a boulder, releasing a stream of air. "When I was little, she'd give me these pep talks, sayin how it was on me to carry the baton, get us to the finish line."

"What happened?" Seed says.

"One day when I was ten," Moses says, "stove wouldn't come on, so I fucked around with the connection in the back but couldn't get it going. Couple hours later some marshal from the gas company evacuates the building, sayin a gas leak been reported. Outside, I tell the dude I'd been messing with the stove, so he goes back in, comes out a few minutes later, looks at me, says, 'You trying to blow up the whole block?'"

Moses pauses, pulls in a breath. "From that day on, my mom was spooked, convinced I was going to get us all killed, and she backed off, left me alone."

"Sometimes," Tommy says, "I think my parents would have been better off if they didn't have me."

"Can't stop them biological urges," Connie says.

"It's like I'm the one keeping all their shit tied together," Tommy says.

"You mean, they worry more cause they have a kid," Connie says.

"My grandmother was half Coeur d'Alene, half white," Hotah says. "Grew up in Idaho, used to tell us stories, most of which she made up. I'd always ask, 'Is that real or made up?' and she'd just say, 'You tell me.'

"She told this one story," Hotah continued, "about when the world was young and every winter the Coeur d'Alene women would cry and cry because they couldn't keep their children warm, the Great Salt Lake back then a hundred times bigger, filled with the tears of crying women."

"Lake Bonneville," I say. "Largest paleolake in the Great Basin."

"One day," Hotah says, "Coyote brought deer and buffalo pelts for the whole village and, everyone warm and comfortable, the women stopped crying. But then, by the end of the winter, they were so busy asking Coyote to bring them more furs, and other things, they forgot how to cry. The lake began to dry up, but the women only worried about what Coyote would bring, and as the lake disappeared they worried more, and soon they were begging Coyote to bring water. But Coyote was busy helping other people. And now there is nothing left of the women's tears but a layer of salt on the valley floor and lines on the mountains, *worry lines*, that show how high the lake used to be."

"So which was it?" Muzzy asks. "A real story or made up?"

"I asked some Couer d'Alene elders one time at a cousin's wedding and they said they'd never heard it," Hotah says.

"So she created it," says Muzzy.

"Drip drip," Connie says, and I reach over, swipe his palm.

"Shit swingin back," I say, then to the others, looking at us confused. "Y'all dripping your colors on the woman," I say, "*storytelling* colors."

"But by replacing the Cuoer d'Alene stories with her own," Muzzy says, "she is helping to kill them."

"That story's about the end," says Hotah. "Doesn't matter who's tellin it."

"Speaking of the end," says Connie, "we better see what them chicks are up to."

"Speakin of the *rear* end," says Moses.

One at a time, seven of us clip onto the next cable and zip off toward the next outcropping, after that scrambling down, following Hotah, the moon now higher as we hump through the boulders and brush, reaching the backside of Mount Rushmore, what looks in the half-light like a beaked face on the right side, left side looking like a tangle of reaching arms.

"It's a cool piece of rock," Hotah says. "Especially on this side, where the spirit is still alive."

"I thought your ancestors were buried here," Connie says.

"The mountain is our ancestor," Tommy says.

"Now you know why we got no vertical on the hoop court," Hotah says.

"And why we're so hard to get rid of," Tommy says.

"Always hard to get rid of what was already there," Moses says.

"Other thing y'all don't get," Hotah says, "is how a mountain can have a spirit."

"Cause we so busy lookin through that microscope," Moses says, "breakin shit down."

"Like splitting the atom," I say. "Can't ever put it back together."

"That what you guys doing with this *Unseeding America* trip?" Tommy asks. "Trying to put some shit back together?"

"Nah," Moses says, "That train done left the station."

"Horse done left the barn," Connie says.

"The falcon too," Muzzy says, and we all look at him. "He cannot hear the falconer," he says.

"Where'd you get that?" I say.

Muzzy raises his phone with a grin. "I found that poem the old man on the bus was talking about," he says.

"Okay," I say, "horses, trains, falcons. Time to let em all go free."

As we make our way around the mountain, we hear the whir of power tools, can barely see in the moonlight, plus illuminated patches from what look to be miner's helmets, the women have set up rows of scaffolding, and we stop and watch a mass of bodies swarming over the rock dome, chicks ascending on ropes, crosslines, some on belay, the entire monument covered with bodies, bees swarming honeycomb, locusts devouring leaves.

"Doing what you do best, ain't you boys?" Hellcat has appeared, connected to a line.

"Studying?" I say. "Yes, we are some smart motherfuckers."

"Watching," Hellcat says. "Letting others do the work."

"Damn," Moses says, "wasn't for us, none of y'all'd even be here."

"Oh that's right," Hellcat says, "you the prophet set us free, delivered that speech on Black Elk Peak—I heard about you and Little Man up there. Like y'all done led us to Mount Sinai. Tell me, Mr. Prophet Man, was it you that birthed each one of these children, taught em to breathe, give em the gift of ambulation?"

"*What?*" I say.

"Ambulation, walking," Hellcat says. Then back to Moses, "That what you did, give em the *hunger* to leave where they was and join the migration? You give em the air in they lungs?"

"Just saying we pointed the way," Moses says.

"The way where? To Mount Rushmore?"

"Toward the open space," he says.

"You didn't *point* to anything. You went, we went. That's how things happen, Moses. Cause you in front for one millisecond don't mean you leadin. More like you bein pushed from behind. Hell, half us took a southern route to get here—ain't followed nobody. We all goin the same place, that's all."

"This where we're goin?" I say. "Mount Rushmore?"

Hellcat looks at me cockeyed. "Don't fuck with me, Little Man." Her eyes shimmer in the moonlight. "Playin dumb," she says, shaking her head.

I can't help but smile. "Sometimes not knowing where you're going is fun."

"You ain't never not known nothin," she says.

"No difference any way," Moses says. "Tween knowin and not knowin."

"Cause we either goin or we ain't," Hellcat says.

"Where?" I say. "Going where?"

This time Hellcat leans back and hoots, at that exact moment someone grabbing my neck and swinging around me from behind, Sheila, connected to the same line as Hellcat, her cheeks and shoulders covered in white powder.

"They ain't standin roun doin nothin," Hellcat says to Sheila, "they *studyin.*"

"We just about done anyway," Sheila says, leaning close, giving me a peck on the cheek with powder-coated lips.

"How'd you deal with Security?" I ask her.

"What that *GoFund* account for," Sheila says.

Sheila pivots away, leaps into the air, and slides back toward Rushmore, Hellcat pushing off in pursuit.

Moon setting in the west, sky along the eastern rim beginning to lighten, Hotah leads the group around to the front of Rushmore, and I stay behind, standing on a granite outcropping, telling them I'll catch up.

Facing east, I lower my butt to the stone, looking past Rushmore to the pink creeping over the horizon, the rosy-fingered dawn. Who the hell said that? Shakespeare? Homer? Huckleberry Finn?

I sit watching the sun reach its fingers into the sky, pulling itself up from its slumber, little by little showing its egg-yolk orange face, watching not with appreciation, not with wonder. I get that wondering, pondering, conjecturing, provides comfort, release from the burden of not knowing, from the worry that only gets worse, but it's a reaction to the world to which I belong, a separation from it, and seems like the more you wonder, the more you worry.

The rosy fingers fade as the sun clears the horizon, shooting fiery rays across the land. I stand, stretch, and pick my way around the bending trail, joining Hellcat, Tanika, Sheila, Moses, Seed, Muzzy, Tommy, and Hotah who stand shoulder to shoulder, gazing upon Mount Rushmore gleaming in the light of the new day, each of the four president's faces sanded smooth, features gone—four blank moons looking out over the Black Hills.

17

Crashed on the rooftop of the hardware store in the village of Custer, I wake to the sound of beating drums, see bodies rousing across neighboring rooftops.

I walk to the edge, see Main Street down below closed to traffic, a semi-circle of Indians in traditional outfits on a wooden stage, people milling about, couple concession stands selling food, grills smoking.

Text from Sheila saying girls cleared out before sunrise, it's mostly boys on the rooftops standing, stretching.

Music stops, a woman in jeans and long-sleeve tee stepping up to a microphone beside the drummers, four blank faces of Rushmore visible in the distance.

"Those young folk may have been the tools," she shouts, "but it was *Wakan Tanka* erased those faces!"

Gathering crowd applauds.

"Let them come arrest the Great Spirit," shouts someone below.

The drummers resume, several men draped in white pelts and headdresses mounting the stage and dancing, people below dancing too, heads bowed, one foot tapping and stepping, then the other.

A convoy of about 10 police cars—sheriff SUVs, state troopers—pulls up to the barricade, lights whirling, uniformed officers emerging placing hats on heads, Indians continuing to drum and dance.

County sheriff, dressed like civil war cavalry, thick stripe down grey pants, raises a bullhorn. "We need to speak with the responsible parties."

"Go ahead and speak," the man at the mic says. "The Great Spirit is listening."

Cop turns, talks to another at his side.

"Which *people* are responsible?" cop says into the bullhorn.

"For what?" says the man.

"Vandalizing Mount Rushmore," cop says.

"Must be talking about those father-son sculptors, what was their names?" man says, turning to the woman at his side. "Borglum senior and Borglum junior," he says into the mic. "They been dead a long time."

The woman reaches over, takes the mic. "You realize the interest on our money is growing at more than a million dollars a day."

"You want the responsible parties?" one of the drummers calls out, stepping over to the mic. "I have white blood—my grandfather was white. Take me."

The man removes his headdress, drops it on the stage and descends the stairs, another drummer doing the same, several others in the crowd joining them, walking toward the cops to turn themselves in.

"Time to make that move," Moses says.

Tommy and Hotah say they'll catch up once the dust settles, and Moses leads us down a drainpipe on the backside of the building, kids on other roofs moving to the rear, dropping backpacks to the ground, and descending, piling into the backs of pickups, delivery trucks, Ubers, couple chartered busses back there waiting.

The five of us walk a mile or so before we flag down a UPS truck headed to Casper, Muzzy and me starting out up front with the driver, other three wedging into the narrow aisle between shelves of boxes in back.

Muzzy snaps pics out the open side door of the wide-open plain, the "Thunder Basin National Grassland" sign, some distant prairie dogs, then what appears to be a group of cows.

"Those are buffalo," driver says.

Muzzy begs the driver to stop and runs out into the field to within a hundred yards or so of the beasts, shoots some pics, and runs back.

"American buffalo," he says, showing us the pictures, like we weren't sitting there watching.

We turn west at an intersection, pass a group of kids hitchhiking, then another larger group walking.

"The news," driver says, "is reporting bands of kids clear down to Texas."

"One big band," Moses says, "broken into groups."

"You guys part of it?" driver asks.

"Small part," Moses says.

"Statistically insignificant part," I say.

We continue across the flat brown earth, warm air whipping through the open side door, driver pointing out landforms, gulches and washes, telling us how some days he can watch a thunderstorm march in across the plain for hours before it arrives. He leans forward over the wheel, exhales gazing up at the sky, says once he moved out here from Virginia Beach, he never looked back, not one single time.

Muzzy and I rotate into the back, and I get a text from Bindermaus saying we need to meet, that after our stunt at Mount Rushmore we should all be locked up.

"They gonna need a big-ass facility," I text back. "We got kids heading west from the Canadian border to the Mexican."

"You kids are crossing the line," he says.

"Come on, Binder," I say, "we're high school kids learning about our country, about the legacy y'all left us."

"Little Man, you defaced a national monument."

"Shouldn't a been faced," I text.

"You've only gotten this far," he says, "because of the PowerPoint of your posts I put together and presented to the Board—pictures of students camping in the West Virginia coal mines, stowing away on cargo ships across the Great Lakes. They were very impressed, Little Man, because no one was affected. No *property* was affected," he adds. "They even agreed to deputize Ms. Erebus and grant summer school credit, transferable to any district in the country."

"Tell him keep his credit," Moses says, reading over my shoulder. "This ain't about him. Ain't about the Board."

"Let's meet and work out a plan," Dr. B texts.

"Only if you withdraw the credit option. Ain't doin no tit for tat."

"Little Man," Bindermaus says, "we need to provide justification."

"Ain't about that, dude."

"I've been in touch with your father," he says. "He wants to see you."

"Bullshit," I say.

"Alright," he concedes. "But he and your uncle are planning a trip to Wyoming, so why don't we all meet up?"

"Maybe if they're going anyway," I say, immediately texting Lanny, who says it's true, he and my dad have been planning a trip to Wyoming since before I left, some Shoshone dude from the Wind River Rez with bead work my father's been wanting to see.

"What's in it for you?" I say to Lanny.

"Wyoming is somewhere I've never been," he says.

"Lot of places you've never been," I say.

"But only one Wyoming," says Lanny.

Sun slipping behind the mountains to the west, we get dropped at an exit just outside downtown Casper, gas stations and hotels on one side, a wall of trees, greener, leafier than any we've seen since Rapid City, on the other. Must be hiding a waterway. We enter the trees and descend a bank, come across a gang of kids camped out, continue on to a fast-moving brown river, more kids sleeping on the opposite bank, find the thickest section of trees, and head on up.

We rig our bags into hammocks between the limbs, high enough to see chunks of indigo sky through the canopy of leaves, far enough from the lights of Casper to see the stars blinking on.

"What about your mother, Little Man?" Moses says, stretching out, hands locked behind his head. "Last time we were talking about our families, you managed to skip your turn."

"Haven't heard from her in a while," I say.

"What's that mean?" Moses says.

"Just that her life pulled her in."

"You think she's okay?" Connie asks.

"My uncle fills me in from time to time," I say. "She's doing fine. Better since I left."

"That sounds bad," Muzzy says. "Like you have been abandoned."

"She's following her path," I say. "I'm cool with that."

"You definitely the king of letting go," Moses says, lightly swiping my hand.

"Do you think I should go back to Tunisia?" Muzzy says.

"Dude," I say, "Tunisia's over. New York's over. Center Point's over."

"Only way to get where we goin," Moses says, "is to keep goin."

18

First fingers of light showing in the east, that sun forever reaching after us, trying to sneak up from behind and grab hold, we descend to the ground and look for signs of life in the camp by the river.

We pass by a group of tents, flaps open, couple dudes walking back in boxers from the river, dripping dry, one of them cut like a middleweight, other one reed-skinny, both with arms and torsos covered in tats.

They nod as they pass and Connie asks where they're from. Grand Forks, they say.

"What state?" I say.

"North Dakota," skinny one says.

"How's it been?" Moses asks, referring to their journey down to Casper.

"Fine," says cut one, six-pack of abs like sausage links. "Why you askin?"

"Just checkin," Moses says. "You got enough cash? Got the gear you need?"

"Shit," says skinny boy, "our region got plenty of money. We been ordering paint by the case, and we got a brand new tent."

"North Dakota boys livin large," Connie says.

"Long as we can afford it," Moses says.

"Can't keep up with the money comin in," Connie says. "Had to assign three more regional deputies. We should all be sleepin in motor homes."

"What do you paint?" Muzzy asks the two tat boys.

"Wouldn't call it painting," says the one with the abs.

"More like writing epitaphs," says the skinny one.

"On gravestones?" I say.

Skinny eyeballs Abs. "Let's show em," he says.

The two of them pop into a tent, emerge pulling on jeans, still shirtless, slinging satchels over shoulders, and we follow them back to the road, cross over to a truck stop, through to the back corner where they dump their satchels in the back of an old army jeep, the kind with thin tires and no top.

Tat bros hop in the front, three of us climbing over the side into the back seat, other two, Seed and me, into the storage area in the rear.

"Where'd you get the wheels?" Connie asks.

"Got an Air Force base in Grand Forks holds a yearly auction," Abs, who's driving, says. "Traffic downtown looks like a military convoy, half the town driving jeeps."

We slide out onto the highway, exit onto another one bypassing downtown, head south on a fast-moving two lane, when suddenly Abs jams on the brakes and swerves onto the shoulder.

Car still running, Abs hops out and walks straight into traffic, a tractor-trailer blasting its horn and jackknifing to a stop, cars behind it skidding past on both sides.

Just before the double yellow line, Abs stoops down and picks something up from the road, something the size of a woman's purse, turns and walks back toward the jeep, trucker rolling down his window.

"What are you, crazy?" driver calls.

Abs turns back to him, cupping in one hand what we can now see is a turtle tucked into its shell.

"If you think my life is anywhere near as valuable as this guy's," he calls back, "you're the one who's crazy!"

Abs stops beside the jeep, turns the turtle over, showing us both sides, the dome a dark mottled green, the flat belly a brilliant orange around the shape of what looks like the outline of another turtle.

"A Western Painted," I say. "Didn't think they had em at this elevation."

"We're just low enough," Abs says.

Connie reads from his phone. "Fifty-one hundred feet."

Cradling the turtle in one palm, Abs continues past the jeep to an embankment leading down to a small pond and sets it in the grass.

Five more minutes down the highway, we pull into a parking lot before the Nicolaysen Art Museum.

Abs turns to Skinny. "Show time, my brother."

They each grab two cans of spray paint from the satchel and jog up the walkway to the front of the red block of a building, Abs moving to a windowless wall on the right, Skinny going left, jogging across a small courtyard to a second blank wall, sun just showing itself above.

Abs works in black only, boxy outlines about two feet high, first an F, then an R, Skinny spraying out curvy, rounded letters, filling em in solid black, spraying swooshes of yellow along the edges: W... h ... e ... r ... e ...

Abs finishes first – **FREE THE PAINTINGS!**
— and steps over to the corner and watches Skinny feathering on the last touches of yellow – *Where Art Goes To Die!*

The two shirtless tat-boys run back to the jeep, hop in, and we fishtail in a circle and speed out the parking lot.

"In school," Seed says, once we're back on the highway, "they'd take us to the museum in Cedar Rapids and tell us it was there to preserve history."

"Seal it up in a museum," Abs says, "and take out all the oxygen."

"That's the thing," Moses says. "they always tryin remember dead shit. Like it ain't died for a reason."

"That's why we call em epitaphs," Abs says.

"Mark the graves and say goodbye," says Skinny.

Just before the turnoff for the camp site, Skinny points to a sign for the National Historic Trails Center.

"It's only eight o'clock," he says to Abs.

"Alright," Abs says, shooting us a glance in the rearview. "One more stop, gentlemen, if you don't mind."

Connie reads from his phone:

"The National Historical Trails Interpretive Center is a cultural site that honors the intrepid, westward-migration of American pioneers from 1841 to 1868. With a number of real-life, hands-on exhibits, visitors can share the experience had by more than four hundred thousand men, women, and children as they traveled along the Oregon, California, and Mormon Trails through the freezing temperatures of winter and the unsparing heat of summer—all in the quest for freedom."

"Check it out," Connie says, showing his phone to Moses. "Covered wagons filled with mannequins."

"Look like zombies," Moses says.

"Like Madam Tussauds in Times Square," says Connie.

We turn into the entrance, drive up a hillside into a parking lot, couple other cars there, sun half way up the eastern sky.

Abs peers into his satchel, selects two cans, waits for Skinny to select his, and off they go, up the walkway to the one-story building that sits there like a huge cement block plunked into the hillside, the two of them stopping beside a decorative stone wall before the entrance, about ten feet high.

Abs leans forward, bracing himself, hands on knees, and Skinny tucks his two cans into Abs' waistband, takes two quick steps toward the wall, leaps against it with one foot and back-flips directly onto Abs' shoulders.

Abs tosses up a can of paint to Skinny, who gets to work, spraying an orange background, then, dropping that can and catching another tossed by Abs, begins with long plumes of spray to form the letters.

$$T......H......E......R......E...$$

"Where?" Muzzy says, as Abs shakes and tosses a third can of spray paint up to Skinny.

"Nowhere," Moses says.

"Which is here," Connie adds.

"Often mistaken for somewhere," I chip in.

Skinny continues: $$"I....S..........N....O...$$
$$..T....H.....I......N....G..."$$

"These boys ain't markin . . ." I begin.

". . . they *un*marking," Moses finishes.

"H.......E......R......E."

"Reminds me of that big Indian chick, Sacagawea, at that visitor center," I say.

"They always tryin do some bullshit resurrection," Moses says.

"And Bindermaus sayin we defaced Rushmore," I say.

"Shit," Moses says.

"Shit," says Connie.

"Shit," says Seed.

Three of us turn and look at Muzzy. "I would like a cheeseburger," he says.

Abs and Skinny hop into the car breathing hard, a woman walking briskly after them down the walkway, must have come out of the center. Abs starts the jeep but then sits tight, deciding to let the woman approach.

She's wearing jeans and a burgundy pearl-snap shirt, got a sweep of hair angling across her forehead.

Woman stops beside the jeep. "Why?" she says. "Why target a cultural center?"

Abs stands up on the driver's seat, aims a can of spray paint into the air at his side and sprays three quick lines, two vertical, one horizontal, that for a brief second hang in the air.

"H," Skinny announces, as the paint dissipates in the breeze.

Abs sprays out a circle.

"O," says Skinny, mist hovering, disappearing.

Abs shoots off three more quick lines.

"N..." Skinny says, then, Abs spraying out another circle, "O," and finally, after an elegant flourish from Abs, "R."

"HONOR!" Muzzy proclaims.

The woman stands there looking miffed.

Abs drops back behind the wheel and starts the motor.

"Whose?" the woman asks, Abs shifting the jeep into gear, me reaching a hand to her from the back as we drive off, receiving a reluctant, mystified hand swipe.

"*Whose honor?*" the woman calls.

We sleep through the day, and I rouse at five to see a text from Lanny saying they landed at the Casper airport, need to know where to meet me and Dr. B who's apparently already arrived. I do a quick search online, text him and Dr. B to meet me at Molly's Diner downtown.

Once the boys are up, everybody dunking in the river, passing around a bar of soap, we stroll into town, turn onto the wide Casper Main Street, new chain stores mixed in with family-runs, some with those old-time vertical neon signs that go up along the building past the windows upstairs.

Connie leads us into Molly's, pushes the door open and stands still, sweeping the room with squinty eyes, hand hovering at his hip as if over a six-shooter, then nods to us it's safe to enter, the four of them grabbing an open booth, me continuing on to join my pops, Lanny, and Dr. B. in the corner.

"Damn, boy, did you grow another centimeter?" my old man says as I slide in beside him.

"Might a grown two!" Lanny says, leaning over the table to high-five my dad, then settling back, sipping his coffee, recounting how after texting me, he and my pops met up with Bindermaus at the car rental in Casper, my pops chiming in with details of their flight, how by a stroke of good fortune they got to see the entire Denver airport, walking for their connection all the way from Terminal 1 to Terminal 7, a walk that took a good forty-five minutes, their ignorance—not realizing there was a shuttle—allowing them to see things they otherwise wouldn't have.

"Then on the connecting flight, I ordered a club sandwich," my father says, "and they charged me eleven dollars. And I was like, 'This must be a damn good sandwich!'"

"And it was," Lanny says. "Cause you *paid* for it."

"Makes you appreciate it," my old man says.

"Can't trust anything they give you free," Lanny says.

"Little Man," Dr. B, sitting beside Lanny, says, "we need to talk about winding down this cross-country adventure."

"Not sure how you wind down a exodus," Lanny says, leaning on his elbows, "but I'm all ears."

Bindermaus eyes my dad. "Camilo?" he says.

"What'd you call him?" I say.

"Camilo," my father says to me. "You didn't know my born name?"

"I knew Cammy," I say.

"What'd you think that was short for?" Lanny says.

"I didn't."

"Camilo," Dr G. says, "you have something you'd like to say to Arthur?"

"What'd you call him?" my father says.

Lanny shakes his head, reaches across the table to slap my dad on the arm.

"I knew Little Man," my father says, barely able to contain his laughter.

"I believe," Dr. B. says to me, "your father has something to say to you."

My dad pulls in a breath, composes himself, looks at me, and says, "Little Man, we want you to come home."

"Bullshit," I say.

My dad rolls in his lips and nods his head several times, but when he attempts to speak, the laughter erupts, Lanny grabbing at his stomach and keeling sideways into the aisle.

"I tried, Mr. Mouse," my father says, "I tried."

"Yes you did," Lanny says, the two of them looking at each other and erupting again.

"I thought you were going to take this boy by the hand," Lanny sputters, "sign him up for Little League, buy him a Spiderman lunchbox!"

"Wonder Woman!" my dad cackles. "A Wonder Woman lunchbox!" And Lanny has to lift himself from the table and stagger out to the sidewalk.

Sandwiches and fries delivered, Lanny returns, avoiding eye contact with my father.

"Okay then," Dr. B says to me, "but no more surprises."

"We'll have to see," I say.

"Remember, Little Man, this is a field experience," Dr. B says. "Up until that mess at Rushmore, the Board was very impressed."

Tommy had been posting updates, over four hundred Lakota Sioux with mixed ancestry turning themselves in for their role in the desecration of sacred Indian land, camping out in front of the Sheriff's Headquarters, insisting on absolving themselves of their tainted legacy.

"Another day or two, we'll be across the Continental Divide," I say.

"Highest point in the country," Lanny says.

"Has to do with which way, toward which ocean, the rivers flow," I say.

"Ain't that the Mississippi?" my dad says.

"That's a divider," I say, "but different."

"Once you cross over," my dad says, "how you gonna get back?"

"It's a exodus," Lanny says. "Once they cross the Divide, they don't come back!"

My dad looks at me with pride. "You son of a bitch," he says.

Dr. B asks the waitress for the check, my dad standing, bowing, saying that although such company should be enjoyed as long as possible, he and Lanny need to go see a man about a horse.

"See a Indian about some beads," Lanny says with a wink, and they head for the door.

19

Four AM we join a bus chartered by a gang from the riverbank, shirtless tat bros coming out to say they'll see us down the road, handing Connie a cannister of paint.

"Just in case," says Skinny.

About an hour in, once we've made a pit stop at a Walmart off I-80 to stock up on food and supplies, I snap a pic in the dim dawn light of a sign that says, "Continental Divide, Elevation 7000 feet," and release a long breath, my body shedding, exfoliating, another layer as we begin the long slide down into the Great Basin. I post the photo of the sign and type in, *See You At The Bottom, Motherfuckers!*

Couple hours later, I wake to see other pics and videos have been posted, a kid with a melting ice cube on his palm standing in front of the *Welcome to Glacier National Park* sign, video of a kid leaping into the gaping mouth of the Grand Canyon, second later popping back up from a hidden landing, group of chicks down in Mesa Verde posting a series of pics taken with a flash of them ziplining from a cliff dwelling out into the black night, plus a few of them curled up asleep inside dwellings during the day.

About half the busload gets off in Park City, someone saying there's mad-cool abandoned silver mines chicks been camping out in—"Time you get there they'll be long gone," Seed tells them—

rest of us continuing toward Salt Lake, Connie directing the driver onto an exit ramp, arrow pointing to Emigration Canyon.

"We done left Lewis and Clark," Connie says. "Now we pickin up Brigham Young."

As the bus winds down the canyon, Connie reads us a list of facts about the Mormon pioneers, the perils of their prairie schooner pilgrimage, how Utah wasn't even Utah yet, the area not owned by the United States but Mexico.

"Livin on stolen land," Moses says.

"Only kind we got," I say.

The canyon walls open out beside us and we see the city of Salt Lake below in the distance, beyond it the shimmering blue sheet of the Great Salt Lake. Connie tells the driver to pull over and ten or so of us leave our packs, walk up a short trail, and stop before a thirty-foot tall granite monument, three vest-and-jacket-wearing bronze dudes on top.

THIS IS
THE PLACE

Lower, they got smaller dudes on each side posing above inscribed tablets with information about the Spanish explorers, the Donner party who first forged the trail through the Wasatch, the trappers who helped Brigham's Mormons find a place to settle free of persecution.

"Why is it the ones get chased off," Moses says, "always the ones start the next club won't let nobody in?"

"Hang on," Connie says, and he turns and jogs back to the bus, returning a minute later wearing a harness, carrying a plastic grocery bag filled with shit.

Connie removes a grappling hook from the bag, flings it up where it wraps around the middle dude's, must be Brigham's, ankle. Next, he removes three slices of white bread from the bag and loads them into his mouth, chewing hard, rest of us standing there watching as he clips the line to his harness and starts rope-walking up the monument.

At the inscription two-thirds up, he removes the wad of chewed bread and plasters it into the "T" of "THE," chews up a couple more slices and fills in the "H" and the "E," the chewed cud blending with the light gray stone.

"This is place?" Moses says.

Connie removes his can of spray paint from the bag and, in the now blank space, sprays the letter "A."

THIS IS *A* PLACE.

"Can't argue with that," Moses says, Seed and Muzzy now joining us, snapping photos.

Bus ambles along the foothills, merges onto I-15, and we head south along the Wasatch Front, sliding deeper into the Great Basin. We pass the city of Provo on the left, Utah Lake on the right, Seed taking a look, ducking back into his phone, saying we ought to check out Long Shorts in the Shakespeare Festival.

"Right," Moses says, "then we go see Little Man in the tall man contest."

"See for yourself," Seed says.

We all log in, tap the Staten Island Bros group, see a pic of Long Shorts standing before a stage dressed in black tights and black jacket with a grid of gold buttons on the front.

"Home boy stylin," Connie says.

Post from Long Shorts says, "Dude's in the hospital so I'm taking his place—same part I played in 10th grade. Iago, motherfuckers! Giving the business to Mr. Purity!"

"How they gonna perform a cartoon?" says Connie.

"Not that Iago," Moses says.

"*Othello*," I say. "Play about some black dude, big-time war hero, gets messed up by one of his assistants."

"They had black dudes back then?" Connie says.

Moses stares at him.

"What?" Connie says.

"You think y'all invented black dudes?" Moses says.

"Actually," I say, but Moses raises a hand to stop me.

"You invented the negro," he says, "I give you that." He turns back to Connie. "So where we gon see this betrayin motherfucker?"

"Two hundred three miles straight ahead," Connie says. "ETA 5:25. Show begins at seven."

Connie walks up the aisle to give the driver the address of the festival, and we pop in AirPods, plug in phones to charge, Moses sharing a Spotify list called *Post-Topia*, first song by some dude called PrimeMate smooth, repetitive, lulls me into a sweet half-sleep.

We swingin now
We swingin now
Yeah, we swingin now

Ain't nothin bout is, ain't nothin about isn't

Cause we swingin now
We swinging now
Yeah we swingin now

Ain't nothin bout was, ain't nothin bout wasn't

Cause we swingin now
Yeah we swingin now
Motherfuckers swingin now....

We walk beneath a large post-and-beam entry—*Utah Shakespeare Festival*—and first thing we do is get a cup of mead, nonalcoholic, tastes like root beer. Muzzy sniffs out a fast food pavilion and we sit in a courtyard with burgers and fries, watching the people, half of them dressed like Elizabethans, meandering by.

We buy tickets for *Othello*, kill another half hour wandering the grounds with its tents and foot bridges, Muzzy stopping to pose for a pic with his head and hands in a pillory, find our seats in an open-air theater, stage surrounded on three sides by tiered balconies, a woman coming out in a frilly dress and white coif to introduce the Cedar City Repertory Theater and offer thanks for the understudy who, when one of their lead actors was injured in a car accident, "appeared as a gift from God. He may be a bit young," she says, "but with only two days of rehearsal, he took to the role as if he were born to play it. Now sit back," she says, hands floating out to either side, "and let yourselves fly along!"

"Othello isn't gonna be flyin," I say as the curtain rises, revealing Long Shorts there with another dude.

Long Shorts shoots us a look, and a minute later when Roderigo refers to Othello as "the thick lips," shoots us another.

They continue their Shakespearean chit-chat till Iago, in a scene with Desdemona's father, turns and bellows, as much to the audience as to the dude on stage, "A black ram is tupping your white ewe!"

"Boy hammin it up," Connie says.

"He ain't hammin," Moses says.

Iago continues to ensnare every single sucker in the play, from Othello's lieutenant to his own wife, again warning Desdemona's old man about Othello's lusty intentions, saying, "Because we come to do you service and you think we are ruffians, you'll have your daughter covered—" pausing here, again turning to the crowd—"with a Barbary horse!"

Afterward, we find Long Shorts in an enclosed courtyard behind the stage, give him bro-hugs.

"You fucked those dudes up," Seed says.

"Othello went down hard," Connie says.

"The great story," Muzzy offers. "We say in Arabic *'qutil bisilahih.'* 'Destroyed with his own weapon.'"

"Hoist on his own petard," I say, the others looking at me till I shrug. "I listened in class," I say.

"Till you didn't," says Connie.

Just then, I notice Moses has slipped the group, catch Connie's eye.

"Minute before the end," Connie says, "right when Othello stabbed himself, he said he was goin to the bathroom. Dude didn't look right."

"Why you tryin kill a black dude?" Connie asks Long Shorts.

Long Shorts shrugs, offers an empty smile.

"Which way did he go?" Muzzy asks.

We walk back beneath the entryway to the main road, locate the bus, grab our backpacks from the overhead racks, Moses' pack already gone.

We look left to a traffic light and signs for I-15, then right, see another traffic light, beyond it mountains.

"What mountain range is that?" I ask, and Connie checks his phone.

"Black Mountains," he says.

I pull in a long breath, slowly release it. "Alright," I say, "let's go find our prophet."

20

The foothills begin just outside Cedar City, more mid-sized town than city, and we move from a dead-end street onto a trail that leads southeast, walking along a series of gradual switchbacks carved into the first tier of mountains, cresting a ridge where the forest gives way to a dome of tannish-pink slick rock, continue toward another front of mountains with a skirt of conifers.

As the sun dips below the ridge line, we reach a stand of black pine rising above piñon and mesquite, decide to set up camp on the silty black soil, no need to get up in the trees, already at 6,000 feet.

Seed and Muzzy round up branches, start a fire, and we break out the bread, peanut butter, and jelly, Muzzy spearing a sandwich with a twig and roasting it till the bread is charred, peanut butter dripping into the flames.

"My family would use almond butter and honey on tabouna," Muzzy says.

"Where your parents now?" Seed asks.

"My mother lives again with her family. My father is in Tripoli driving the taxi."

"You ever try to contact them?" Connie asks.

"I did," Muzzy says. "But the imam in Fort Wayne told me, 'The reason they sent you here was so you won't ever need to look back.'"

"That's the American dream right there," Seed says.

"Boy dreamin alright," Connie says. "Dreamin bout Big Macs."

"My old man stayed skinny by smoking cigarettes," Seed says, "always saying how cancer is just another item on the menu, every bit as good as obesity and heart disease."

"Echebbi said that which brings you life also brings you death," says Muzzy.

Couple more toasted sandwiches cut into quarters, and we curl up in our sleeping bags, with the absence of other people, of society, no longer having shit to avoid during the day, gradually slipping into synch with the sun rather than going against it.

The chill of night in the high desert settling over us, I slide deeper into my bed roll, think of the popcorn I used to drop off the Chelsea Peer, how I'd watch it slowly work its way against the incoming waves out into the river, going against one force only meaning you're riding a stronger one you can't see.

"You think he's out here?" Connie whispers to me.

"Moses?" I say. "Where else he gonna be?"

Next day packing up, we see a group of dudes approaching, bodies fanned out across the slickrock.

Long Shorts, back in his denim clam-diggers and Confederate hoodie, morning temp still cool, reaches us first, followed by Paisley and three other dudes from Staten Island.

"I was acting," Long Shorts says, first thing. "It was a play."

"Ole Shakespeare," I say. "Some of the shit he writes is so strong it breaks right on through."

"Nah man," Long Shorts says. "That dude was a Moor, from North Africa. It's completely different."

"North African, sub-Saharan, doesn't matter," I say. "You called him just about every animal in the kingdom."

"Nothing ever gets better," Seed says.

"Already had that Big Bang," I say. "All we're doin now is ridin it out."

"So you're saying, 'Seize the day,'" Paisley says.

"Ain't about seizin," Connie says, "it's about *un*seizin, givin the shit back."

Connie extends a hand for Seed to swipe, but Seed doesn't see him, standing there gazing off, others of us tracking his gaze, past the stand of pine trees to the mountain of rock rising beyond.

Saying he saw a figure slip away over the edge, Seed leads us up and over a sheer face, which opens out onto another flat, empty plateau, and fifteen minutes later we're winding our way down a couloir into a bone-dry creek bed, snowpack run-off gone now it's the end of August.

One of the Staten Island dudes calls up from the rear that he scored some weed from some Mormon dude in Cedar City, if anyone would like to join him. Long Shorts and Paisley drift on back, then Muzzy too, Seed staying on point, Connie and me close on his heels.

Seed stops, peering ahead, but I don't see anything.

"Must have been a black ghost," he says.

"Got em in the Amazon basin," I say, "not the Great Basin. Black Ghost Knifefish."

"Yo Iago!" Connie calls back. "Dude's not a ram or a horse. Dude's a knifefish!"

"A what?" Long Shorts says.

"Knifefish," Connie says. "Some kind of slithering creature comin get you!"

"Black panther," Seed says.

"A black wolf," calls Muzzy.

"*Melanistic* wolf," I say.

Paisley, lookin a little glazed, steps up to the front. "The darker the berry, the sweeter the juice," he says.

"Yo Iago," I call back to Long Shorts, "why you tryin torture that black dude?"

"You saw the play," Long Shorts says.

"Somethin bout bein passed up for a promotion," Connie says.

"Just wonderin why you had to go all 'black ram,' 'barbary horse' on his ass," I say.

"People take any difference and turn it into a sign of evil," Muzzy says.

"Dude *was* awfully black," I say.

"A black stallion," Seed says.

"Black mamba," says Connie.

"Amazonian knifefish," I say.

"Othello or Moses?" Paisley asks.

Connie, Seed, and I answer together, "Both."

We continue on into the afternoon, down into another arroyo that opens out into a mottled rockscape of pink Navajo sandstone.

"Red rock reminds me of Midès," Muzzy says.

"Midès must be on Mars," says Seed.

Connie gets a single bar and we wait for his map to load.

"Dude may have been aimin for the Black Mountains," Connie says, "but what he got was the Dixie National Forest."

Connie passes his phone around and, sure enough, the floating blue dot is just past the northern boundary of the Dixie National Forest, just above Zion National Park.

We continue through a stand of pine trees down into a ravine, sun rising higher, getting stronger.

"Welcome to the southland," says a voice.

Straight above us, perched on the edge of the canyon wall, is Moses.

"Damn, bro," Connie calls to him, "we tryin leave you behind!"

"I believe it," Moses says, barely loud enough for us to hear.

"What happened?" I call. "Iago give you the spooks?"

"Should a gone back with Smiley when I had the chance," Moses says.

"Cause each step forward takes you in deeper," Connie says.

Moses stands, wriggles into his backpack, and disappears beyond the ridge.

Seed leads us up a slim ledge along the wall, passing within twenty feet of a pair of unimpressed bighorn sheep, and we reach the top and see before us an expanse of darker red sandstone.

"From the fryin pan to the fire," Connie says.

We cross the slickrock, Long Shorts, Paisley and the others trailing along, Seed leading us down into a narrow gulley, walls overhanging, forming a nearly enclosed tunnel beneath a curving snake of blue sky.

We pick our way past a couple of small pools, and the tunnel opens out into a dirt-clay gulch with a large green pond surrounded by trees, north-facing wall coated in moss.

Seed and Muzzy strip down and wade into the pond where it's waist-high, Connie and me standing by as they dive and emerge, dive and emerge, till we say what the hell and join them.

"Y'all new baptized!" Moses calls, and we look up from the water to where he's sitting, legs dangling over the edge of the sheer wall.

"Come join us!" I call.

"Nah man, this shit don't wash off."

"You're talkin that bible shit, that curse of Ham shit," Connie calls.

"That's right," Moses calls. "If we can't outrun the shit, must be carryin it with us. Ain't that right, Long Shorts?"

Long Shorts stands there in the green water.

"What's up with that?" Connie says to Long Shorts. "First, you're bragging about your Confederate hoodie, then you're chillin with them Trinidad dudes, then you're taking down Othello. Which way you playin it, Homes?"

Long Shorts shrugs.

"You ain't the only one carryin this Dixie National Forest!" I call to Moses. "Whatever you're carrying, we are too."

"Always seein the big picture, ain't you, Little Man?" Moses says. "Maybe it's time you come down to earth and explain this pilgrimage you leadin."

"*I'm* leading?" I say. "That's what this three-day march into Dixie's about? Feelin some doubt, Moses? Missing your moms? Bindermaus? School?"

"This about us, Little Man. Shit I left behind is behind. This about who's going forward from here. Bout how many Iagos we got."

"We done crawled most of the way across the country," I call up to him, "and you see one play, written four hundred years ago, and want to drag us right back where we started."

"Now you doin that age-old shit, sayin the dude see the problem the one caused it. Nah, man, I ain't playin that. You need to come clean, once and for all."

I hold my hands out to either side, not sure what to say. I turn to Long Shorts.

"What?" he says.

I keep looking at him.

"Want me to go up there?" he says.

I half shrug, half nod.

Long Shorts loads on his backpack, walks over to the cliff face, and begins to climb, Moses leaning forward to watch him.

The wall is near 90 degrees, one section halfway up actually steeper, Long Shorts reaching up and back onto an overhang, clinging like a spider.

We watch Long Shorts reach Moses on the ledge, pull himself up, two of them standing a moment facing each other, saying something we can't hear, then disappearing together beyond the ridge.

Rest of us find a patch of trees in black soil, lay out our bags and blankets, break out the remaining food, Muzzy and Seed rounding up wood for a fire.

After half a toasted PB&J, sun nearing the peaks of the two sandstone domes to the west, I wander off, seeking higher ground to get some perspective. I head up a slope to the east, find a loose boulder to sit on, having outpaced the descending sun which now sits higher, ten degrees or so above the sandstone humps.

Inevitable, I guess, that Moses would run out of gas at some point, be overtaken by gravity. Easy for me to preach weightlessness. Tell everyone to just let go.

Cause of my mother and father, I suppose, Lanny, circumstance, cause of my own particular neuro wiring. Plus, factor in the historical moment—I mean, I know how history works, know I'm not part of it, we're not. I know about the aftermath. How sometimes shit just needs to run its course.

But it doesn't ever break cleanly, and whatever we're leavin behind, whatever unfinished business we've got, someone's got to carry it. No matter where you go, you've got to look back. Somebody does.

I think of what Connie and I said to Landscape, how chill he was when we offered our explanation, telling him the shit was starting to swing back the other way, us not going with the light but with the dark energy. How the visible world is nothing but a reciprocal, or refracted, version of the invisible world, light the visible edge of darkness, the world itself nothing but a hardened nugget, not made by forces pushing in but by those pushing out, specs of matter bursting forth from nothingness.

The sun dropping behind the mountains, I walk higher up the slope, countering the sun's descent, climb onto an outcropping and jump across a gap onto a larger spire, continue up on all fours to the top where I sit and allow the fireball to again sink toward land.

As the sun touches the tip of the mountain on which Moses and Long Shorts will apparently be spending the night, I feel an urge swelling inside, an urge not to know or understand, not even to connect—no, loneliness is the knife edge of absolute belonging—but to let go that last little bit, cut that last thread keeping me connected.

But then, again, the thought we may be losing Moses, he may not be able to step out of the quicksand that's got him, and a current of fear courses down my spine.

I know we can't go on without him.

Fear burning from the inside out, I raise myself to a stand, my organs opening out to the world like a bloody flower.

"Moses!" I call. "*Moses!*"

In the morning, we rouse with the rising sun, no longer racing from it, well beyond the continental divide, see Moses and Long Shorts above, sitting on the ledge.

Moses stands in the low streaming sunlight, calls down they'll meet us on the backside at the trailhead he took up there, and half hour later we reach the two of them, Long Shorts in his Confederate flag hoodie.

"So?" Connie asks.

Two of them look at each other, then back at us.

"I forgave him," says Long Shorts.

"*You* forgave *him?*" says Seed. "For what?"

"For not forgiving me," Long Shorts says.

We stand there, thinking there might be more, but that's it.

"Okay then," Connie says, "long as everybody good."

"Ain't said nothin bout good," Moses says, eyes sparkling. "But nobody ever got to the end sittin around wonderin."

21

Moving southwest through the canyon, which descends into a steep, narrow gorge then opens out again, we hear a cry, some sort of warbling whimper, look up and see a pair of heads bobbing above the ridge, then nothing.

Another half mile down the canyon, we hear the sound of trickling water, climb up on a shelf and follow a wide rock-strewn chute up to a walkway with chain railing and tourists in sunhats and fanny packs. We hear another high-pitched whimper, keep walking, hear another one, Connie saying he's got two bars, checking his map, reporting we're approaching Weeping Rock.

"That's a rock making that noise?" asks Seed.

"Weeping refers to the dripping water." Connie points ahead to a towering, glistening overhang, lichen and moss growing out of hairline fissures in a blend of green, brown, yellow.

Rangy one leads us up another steep chute, around the overhang to a plateau on top where we stop before two black-haired chicks on barrel-chested horses, few more approaching from the rear.

One of the two horses shuffles its feet, releases a chortling whinny, same sound as the whimpers we heard.

Sheila and Hellcat ride up and stop beside the first two, Hellcat on a large brown mare, Sheila's a spotted Appaloosa.

"This Weeping Rock?" Hellcat asks.

"Nice to see you too," says Moses.

"We rode two hundred miles to pay our respects," Hellcat says. "Ain't come to chit-chat."

"Figured that shriekin had to be women," Moses says.

"That time of the month," I say, throwing Moses a hand swipe.

"Ain't about no month, Little Man," Hellcat says.

Hellcat coaxes her horse a couple steps further to where, craning forward, she can see down to the water seeping out from the cracks onto the overhang.

"Rode from Grand Junction," Sheila says. "Four days and nights, these two Indians leadin, tellin us how the cryin's over, only tears left comin from this mountain."

"Must a heard that story bout the lakes dryin up from Hotah's grandma," I say.

"Probably got their own stories," Moses says.

"We all livin in the same world," Sheila says.

"Echebbi says when we forget our stories, we die," Muzzy says.

"Forget our what?" I say.

"Our stories."

"Our *what?*" says Moses.

Couple other women arrive, and seven in total dismount their horses, two of them removing leather cords from saddlebags, weaving them through the rings of the horses' bits, handing the end of one to Seed, other one to Connie.

Women walk down the chute to a small ledge on the face of Weeping Rock, gather rivulets of water in cupped hands, splash it on their faces, and return.

"Where you going now?" I ask.

"Down," Hellcat says, as they mount their horses, turn back the way they came.

"Down where?" asks Connie.

"Got us a luxury suite in the devil's parlor," Hellcat says, walking off, their pack disappearing beyond the ridge, us boys standing watching until they reappear in the arroyo below Weeping Rock, slowly moving west.

Connie looks up from his phone, Moses at his side leaning against the window.

"Lot of motherfuckers in Vegas," Connie says. "Must be hittin the slots, cause they withdrawing a shitload of money."

"But they cannot gamble," Muzzy says, one row back. "They are too young."

"They ain't gambling," Moses says. "Not what this trip's about."

"Well, they spending money like gamblers," Connie says. "*Unlucky* gamblers."

Nine that evening, just getting dark, I wake to see we've left the interstate and are cruising past huge sparkling hotels, throngs of pedestrians on the sidewalks, at every corner two or three kids manning tables made of crates, cardboard boxes, loose boards. We get off at a glowing pond, illuminated from within, in front of the Bellagio, check out the fountain pulsing up in the shape of a giant harpsichord, water changing color in time to music from in-ground speakers, and stroll on up the sidewalk.

"This place is lit," Seed says.

"Ha!" says Muzzy.

We come to the first table of kids, pedestrians milling around, chick at the table wearing a violet crew-neck sweater, hair cut in a perky bob.

"Little Man, Moses," chick says, recognizing us, "tell these people about reverse gambling."

"When people win instead of lose?" I say.

"Exactly," she says. "That's the point of the fund you started—is that Connie there? Hey Connie—to always have more than you need."

"Cause it ain't about money," says Connie, stepping forward.

"Can't take it with you!" says perky Jane.

"Tonight," announces a dude seated beside Jane, rainbow-dyed scruff on his chin, "everybody leaves with something!"

"Is it legal, giving money away?" asks one of the crowd.

"We're not giving it away," says Jane. "You have to win it!"

"How do we play?"

"You *are* playing!" says Jane. "You just won fifty dollars!" She removes a wad of bills from her shoulder bag, peels the guy off a 50.

"They're giving us back the money we lost," another pedestrian says.

Jane steps onto the makeshift table, a board placed upon a couple of melon crates. "Ladies and gentlemen!" More people stop, turn to see. "Come get your gift from the *Unseeding*, or as we like to call it, the *Paying it Back Tour of America!*" Jane bends forward to hear a question from someone, then straightens. "Because we don't need it!" she bellows.

"Tonight you're playing with house money!" calls Mr. Scruff.

Jane stands there a moment beaming at the crowd of listeners, then hops down to the sidewalk and, with a couple others herding people into a line, sits on her stool, a large wooden spool without the cable, doling out fifties.

We continue up the strip, lines growing at each corner table.

"Check it out," Moses says, eyeing a woman with her child, two of them stepping onto the end of a line. "She just got her money and went right back on line."

Moses steps over to the woman, rest of us following. "Excuse me, Mam," Moses says. "I noticed you getting on line a second time."

Woman doesn't answer, just pulls her daughter in close and turns away.

"I want to be sure your daughter knows what courage that takes," Moses says.

Woman shoots Moses a quick glance, shifts her position, gives him the other shoulder.

"You've got a brave mother," Moses says to the girl, face hidden behind her mother's forearm. "Well tonight," Moses says to the mom, "you hit the jackpot."

Moses pulls a crumple of bills out of his pocket, smooths out three hundreds, couple of fifties, steps around the child and hands it to the woman, who takes it, avoiding eye contact, muttering something to her daughter, stepping forward to keep her place in line.

Reminds me of the time in 8th grade I got detention for not saying thank you when the assistant principal brought a tray of Christmas tree cookies to my homeroom. Made us get on line, handed me a cookie and said, "What do you say, Little Man?" and when I shrugged, he got pissed, stood up from the desk and lectured the class about how our lack of gratitude would be our undoing.

Seemed to me that by not saying anything, I was letting the gesture stand on its own, unhitched to anything I might say, my attention where it was supposed to be, on the cookie.

"Whose honor?" I say to my boys, echoing the woman at the Historic Trails Center. "Right there," I say, the woman and child moving up the line. "That's whose."

22

Back on the bus at 3 a.m., some kids have returned, new ones taking the places of those that have not. The driver, roused from a nap, claps his hands together, talks with Connie a moment, and cranks up the motor, Connie returning to his seat beside Moses in front of me, telling us we'll be at the bottom in a couple hours.

"Death Valley?" Moses says.

"Lot of kids already there," Seed says, sitting with Muzzy across the aisle, scrolling through the latest posts.

"What will we do in Death Valley?" Muzzy asks.

"Sweat," Seed says.

"Roast," I say.

"Till all your sins are burned away," Connie says.

"What if you have no sins to burn?" Muzzy asks.

"Throw your ass in the devil's frying pan," Moses says, "I guarantee somethin gon sizzle."

We pass through Death Valley Junction, on to a ranger station, Connie and me going in to pay the fee, ranger telling us that with the deluge of young people they've been instructed to waive the entry fee, man the stations 24 hours a day, make sure we have enough water, dude saying the governor is keeping tabs, doesn't want anything to go wrong now that we've reached California.

Ranger leads us to a tractor-trailer out back stacked full of boxes, four jugs of water in each, telling us this is the third truckload, kids arriving all day, in busses, trucks, cars, on motor scooters, skateboards . . .

Connie and I each grab a box, send back the others for more, load them into the bus's luggage compartment, and we rumble on through the filtered light of breaking day till Connie asks the driver to stop in a parking area, where we pull on backpacks and sidle out the door, a dark line of hills on one side, on the other, Badwater Basin, an open expanse that looks like a brown lake with a patch of ice in the center.

We pass over the white patch, and I lick a finger, dab it, and taste. "Salt from a million years of evaporated lakes," I say.

"Million years of women's tears," Moses says.

The morning air is cool and we head south a quarter mile or so to a spot beside the Funeral Mountains of the Amargosa, curl up in our bags and blankets to get some sleep.

I wake in the late-morning heat, shade from the mountains sucking away beneath the rising sun, sit up, look out over the basin, reddish-brown, barren, lunar, sit there with the others asleep at my side, and watch the sun slow-roast the earth.

One bar on my phone, I wait for the latest posts to load, first one a selfie of Hotah the night before leaning out the window of Tommy's pickup, hair blowing back in the wind, over his shoulder a sign for the Continental Divide, Hotah's caption saying, "California Dreaming!"

I send a text to Sheila who responds that they're working their way down through Nevada.

"You know the way?" I ask, unsure how they're navigating through the back-country, probably with little to no phone coverage.

"The way to the bottom?" Sheila says. "How bout you take a break from the stupid pills, Little Man?"

Moses and Connie wake up, and we drape white t-shirts over our heads and hike up into the mountains, find a spot to sit and watch the new arrivals entering Badwater Basin, in groups, as individuals, small black insects lugging their loads, smaller groups joining larger groups, inching south toward the Funerals.

"Indians at three o'clock," Connie says, a red pickup pulling into the parking area between a couple of busses.

Tommy and Hotah exit the truck with backpacks and join the procession through the heat—at noon, it's a hundred degrees—looking for shade in the folds of the mountains, some continuing past us up the trail to make camp at Dante's View where it's cooler, rangers allowing it cause the regular campgrounds are overloaded, Muzzy and Seed intercepting Tommy and Hotah, leading them back to our spot where they swipe our hands and drop their packs.

Second day, we watch for over an hour a group of horses walk slowly toward us across Badwater, and another fifteen minutes up the trail to reach us.

Hellcat swings herself down from the brown mare.

"Who else you gon see ridin a tamed beast in the eighth circle of hell?" she says, giving my shoulder a squeeze, turning back to the others. "This a homecoming for us, right ladies?"

Tanika swings her long legs off her horse, then Sheila, five other girls sitting tight.

"You runnin little low on dark energy, Little Man?" Sheila says. "Ain't even up to sea level here."

"I guess three thousand miles'll take some of the air out," I say.

"You just missing me," Sheila says.

"What I want with a pufferfish?" I say.

"Then you bes stop dangling that worm-bait," she says, sending a gentle backhand into my crotch.

Sheila leans in, pushes her dry lips against my own, when she pulls back our bottom lips momentarily sticking together. She eyes me, then again leans in, the two of us standing there in front of the others, Sheila working her mouth against mine until the kiss becomes a slavering, sloppy mess.

"There," she says.

"Smiley got a ticket to Vegas," Tanika says to Moses. "Coming in tonight."

"Believe it when I see it," Moses says.

"Alright girls," Hellcat says, "let's leave these boys to their purgatory and get back to the hotel."

"Hotel?" Muzzy says.

"You tell em," Hellcat says to Hotah, remembering him from Black Elk Peak, "bout how we done our time in Badwater."

"You talking about the story he told us from his grandmother?" I say. "How do you know about it?"

"It's a story bout me, Little Man, bout my tears," Hellcat says. "I *heard* it."

Hotah points to the white patch of salt on the valley floor. "There they are," he says.

Hellcat swings onto her horse and leads the pack at a walk down the trail, back across Badwater Basin toward Furnace Creek.

Dudes continue trickling into the valley, rangers at the road directing chicks on to the hotels, which they've reserved, probably weeks ago, Sheila posting pics that afternoon of The Oasis, two-level stucco hotel with terra cotta roof and an hour glass swimming pool surrounded by a grove of palm trees, chicks camping out on the grounds, others posting from different hotels, girls overflowing into lobbies, conference rooms, curled up on carpeted floors, in the cushioned booths of restaurants.

"I would like to stay in a hotel," Muzzy says, seven of us sitting on our perch munching PB and Js.

"Oh yeah?" Moses says. "Kick back in a Holiday Inn, get you a couple burgers, watch some HBO?"

"Yes," says Muzzy.

"What part of 'paying it back' don't you understand?" Moses asks him.

"I have never taken anything. I came from Tunisia."

Moses stares at him. "Listen," he says, "You want to feel cheated, you got every right."

"It was a cool experiment," I say, "that whole life and liberty thing. But it's over."

"It wasn't my experiment," Muzzy says.

"Nah man," Moses says. "You may have been so far back you couldn't see the locomotive, but you was pulled along just like everybody else, peasant farmers in China to taxi drivers in Tripoli."

"God damn," Connie says.

Rest of us turn to see a figure climbing through the heat-haze toward us in a tan fedora, backpack slung over one shoulder.

"No way," Moses says, and a minute later Smiley reaches us, looking if not taller, definitely slimmer.

"Work I did with my mama got to count for somethin," he says, dropping his pack.

"Devil don't care what route you take," Moses says, "long as you show up."

"In proper attire, no less," Connie adds.

Smiley removes the fedora, holds it out. "Bumped into Lanny at Pablo's," he says, eyes shifting to me. "Told him I was going back to meet y'all, and he took the hat off his head and give it to me."

Smiley steps over and swipes my hand.

"How is your mother?" Muzzy asks.

"Dead," Smiley says. "Tanika wanted to come home, but she wouldn't let her. Long as she had one of us with her. Said Tanika's job was to *represent*."

"I am sorry," Muzzy says.

"Every day, I cooked her meals," Smiley says, "cleaned her bedpan. Before she died, she said to me. 'I didn't know if it was you holding on or me, but I'm glad you came back.'"

Moses walks over, offers a hand which Smiley softly swipes.

"Tomorrow," I say, "we check out that Badwater salt."

"What's there?" Smiley asks.

"Your mama's tears," Moses says.

23

Strewn throughout the lower folds of the Funeral Mountains, bodies of boys, one by one, stir to life as the shade draws back beneath the climbing sun. From the fiery red Panamint Range to the west, more bodies rouse and move in, while new arrivals continue to enter from the mouth of the basin to the east, slowing as they approach, sun nearing its apex, kids dripping sweat, some with white t-shirts, or shorn sections, tucked Arab style under baseball caps, most everyone toting gallon-sized water jugs.

The eight of us walk out to the center of the salt flat, hard as asphalt, stand still as a crowd gathers.

"Hundred fifteen degrees!" Connie announces, crowd thickening, swelling out on all sides, some settling down onto the hot earth.

"Hundred sixteen!" Connie calls out.

"And that's in the shade," Moses mutters.

"What shade?" says Seed, settling himself onto the ground, rest of us joining, except Moses.

Moses rotates in a circle, stops, stamps a foot down against the crusted surface of salt, and the murmuring of the crowd fades to silence.

"There's a story been told about these tears," Moses says, speaking at volume, glancing at Hotah. "We ain't come here to build nothin up or tear nothin down. We here just to be here."

Moses turns to me, his forehead shining wet, and I stand, sweat trickling down my scalp, dripping off my nose.

"Hundred eighteen!" Connie calls.

Moses lowers himself to the ground and the eyes of the crowd shift to me.

"Where we goin today?" I ask, my voice soft, only kids nearest able to hear.

"Nowhere," a few answer.

"Where we goin today?" I ask again, my voice stronger.

"Nowhere!" answers the crowd.

With great effort—it's a hundred eighteen in the shade, where there is no shade, at 280 feet below sea level—I lift my right arm from my side, hand clenched into a fist, and lower it, then raise my left fisted hand and right foot together, lower them, raise the right hand and left foot, pumping my arms and legs in a slow rhythm.

After a minute, Moses stands and joins me, the two of us running slow-motion in place, salty sweat dripping into my eyes, others rising, pumping their arms and legs, trapped, ensnared in the heat, bodies dripping sweat onto the ground around their pumping feet.

"One hundred nineteen!" Connie calls out.

Slowly, we continue until everyone in all directions has joined, crowd of boys grown to thousands running in place, sweat pouring from our bodies, adding our own layer of salt to Badwater Basin.

Sun below the ridgeline of the Panamint, we sit in the foothills of the Funerals resting our spent bodies, women arriving on horseback, others shuttling over in busses to treat us with cool compresses, body cream, douse us from jugs of water.

Sheila finds me lying beside a boulder, not as badly sunburned as others, just dehydrated. She rubs lotion into my arms and legs, removes my t-shirt and massages the lotion into my back, her fingers sliding beneath the waist band of my boxers, kneading out the ribbed pattern in my flesh.

"Keep sippin," she says, raising the water to my lips.

Tanika tends to Smiley, Hellcat flitting about, directing girls to boys in need.

The girls, women, whatever—even Hellcat knows we're past that now—stay with us through the night, going for water when we run out, softly singing to those too sunburned to sleep.

In the dim blue light of dawn, they mount their horses, board their waiting busses, and head back to Furnace Creek.

24

One day of recuperation and it's time to continue west, the bottom a destination in its own right, no question, but not to be confused with the end.

At our bus, Connie huddles with the driver, who's in contact with the other drivers, what was thirty or forty of them when we arrived now over a hundred, maybe two hundred, with more empty charters pulling in, word getting out we got another big-ass mountain range to cross, kids done with Tarzanning, hitchhiking, Ubering, leaving motorcycles, Vespas, bicycles strewn like carcasses across the valley floor.

Busses heading out the western exit of the park all morning, ours goes early afternoon, girls' busses zippering into the procession from hotel parking lots.

Connie points out Mount Whitney, announces, "Fourteen thousand five hundred and five feet," Muzzy and me snapping pictures, Moses peering out at the towering peaks, unable to tell which one is Whitney, then drifting off to sleep.

We continue up 395, dozing and waking, turn at Lee Vining, head up into Tioga Pass. I scroll through a couple sites about the Sierra Wilderness, read about John Muir, some quotes about lovely this and natural that, reading one quote a second time: "The power of our imagination makes us infinite." Nah, I think, not really. Only thing makes you infinite is to stop imagining altogether.

"Soon as you think it, you shrink it," I say to Connie, one seat in front.

"Soon as you say it, you slay it," Connie returns.

"Soon as you make it, you take it," Seed chimes in from across the aisle.

"Once you build it, you killed it," says Moses.

I find another quote by Muir, tell the others to listen up.

> There is not in all the Sierra, or indeed in the world, another so grand and wonderful a block in Nature's handiwork, that behooves us to see that these wild mountain parks are passed on unspoiled to those who come after us.

"Something not right," Moses says.

"Because there is a place more wonderful," Muzzy says, "Chebika. Garden of the Tunisian desert."

"The idea of keeping people from spoiling shit is cool," says Connie.

"But for what reason?" Moses says. "Dude sayin so we can pass it on to those who come after us."

"Can't pass on somethin ain't yours," says Smiley. "Don't matter how wonderful."

Moses reaches over, swipes Smiley's hand.

I stand up and call to the back of the bus. "Yo Hotah! That land out there belong to us?"

"I told you at Black Elk," Hotah replies. "We belong to it."

We get the bus driver to pull into a parking area carved into the side of a granite wall, kids filing out, fanning out to pee.

"We in the heights now," Smiley says, zipping up, gazing past the wall into the open vista of mountain tops rising up from evergreens.

"Nine thousand nine hundred forty-three feet," Connie reports.

Hotah and Tommy locate a path beyond the parking area, lead a group of us up along a wash of stone blocks onto a landing beside a hulking granite dome.

"My grandmother used to say that where there's a mountain there are no words," Hotah says.

"Where we come from and where we're going," Tommy says.

"Here's what I don't get," says Seed. "If it's inevitable, the only way it possibly can be, why's the dude sayin it's wonderful?"

"Breathless motherfuckers," Moses grumbles. "Out here singin hosanna same time they fuckin everything else up."

"Yes," Muzzy says, "believing you are going to *Jannah*, Paradise, makes it okay to turn the earth into *Jahannam*, hell."

I keyword "hell on earth" and first thing comes up is a short video of the aftermath of 9/11, the ash covered streets and cars downtown, couple people walking, heads bowed, hands over mouths, passing a soot-faced fireman sitting on a stoop, a stray dog sniffing an ash-coated paper bag.

I pass my phone to the others, who watch the video, hand it back to me, and we turn back to the clouds wisping over the evergreens, sliding between the great mute mountains.

Together, my boys and I stand in silence, breathing deep the thin air, gazing out at the wonderless world.

25

We slide down into Yosemite Valley, gold light flooding the foothills, creating shallow pans of late-afternoon shade. Bus driver waves Connie to the front, Connie seat-paddling up then back, saying the driver needs to take a full hour break, pulling over at the next turn-off, Seed eying his phone, saying we're just leaving Moccasin, next town Chinese Camp.

"Must be where the railroad workers lived," I say.

Connie, also on his phone, says, "Gold, dude. This where a couple grand of Chinese settled during the gold rush."

"Grand?" Smiley, two rows back, says.

"Couple thousand," Connie says.

"Grand mean money," Smiley says.

"How bout K?" Connie says. "Couple K Chinese."

"Alright," Smiley says.

We emerge from the shadowy foothills into the orange light of the valley, bus driver pulling over in front of a small white church, and we file out into a waning day that is getting both hotter with the loss of altitude and cooler with the loss of light.

"Where this church come from?" Smiley says, six of us clustering by the bus as others drift past.

"Same place we all come from," says Moses. "Same place we all goin."

"I liked the pre-prophet Moses," Smiley grumbles.

"Me too," Connie says. "Didn't know shit. Could take a couple steps without seeing the end."

Smiley reaches a hand over to Connie's, and we walk slowly onto the grounds, few kids in the far-side parking lot shooting baskets.

"Seeing the end," Moses says, "shit."

"I remember my old man on that tower looking at your face," Seed says to him.

"Like he some kind of Buddha," Connie says.

"The whole story right there," Seed says.

"Don't mean I knew nothin," Moses says.

"Seed's old man wasn't mesmerized by what you knew," I say, "but by the tonnage of what you didn't."

"That's what I'm sayin." Moses turns onto the pathway toward the church, rest of us following.

"That makes you more wise!" Muzzy calls from the rear, Connie throwing me a look, bracing for some Echebbi. "The *rajul hakim*, the smart man—" Muzzy begins.

"The *wise* man," Connie interjects.

"The *wise* man," Muzzy says, "is the one who can say not what he knows but what he does not know."

"That Echebbi or you readin some dumb-ass meme?" Smiley says.

Muzzy shrugs, not understanding.

"Always got to be about knowin or not knowin," Moses says.

"Being or not being," Connie says.

"Homeboy been readin his Shakespeare," I say.

"You ain't the only one ever open a book," Connie says.

"Know or don't know, be or don't be," I say. "Left or right, with or against. Like the whole world stuck in binary."

"Like we got to divide shit so it make sense," Moses says.

"Male and female," Connie says. "That's why we goin non-binary."

"Nah man," Smiley says, "male and female's okay."

"Nobody sayin it ain't," Moses says. "Connie just saying they overlappin more than separate."

"Y'all unravelling or puttin shit back together?" Smiley says.

"Dog," Moses says, "unravelling *mean* puttin shit back together."

We stroll pass the church and check out the kids shooting hoops, couple boys, one in jeans and t-shirt, other wearing a school uniform, a girl in the same khakis and blue polo sitting on a bench watching. Moses leads us onto the court, takes a rebound, pounds the ball hard against the blacktop and goes up to dunk but can't, ball jamming against the front of the rim.

"You one gravity bound motherfucker," I say to him, and he tries again, same result.

Kid in jeans drifts off, hops on his bike, pedals away.

"Where you from?" Smiley asks the boy in uniform.

"Beijing," he answers.

"According to Wikipedia, ain't no Chinese left in Chinese Camp," Connie says.

The girl, looks older than the boy, walks onto the court and tells us they go to school in nearby Stockton, but are spending the day with their parents who are checking out the area.

"Checking out the history?" Connie asks, suspicious.

"Same thing we doin," Moses says.

"We own the church," the girl says.

"Our parents own real estate company," says the boy, his English not as good. "First to get visa for Shen Shen—" he nods at the girl, must be his sister—"then company start to grow."

"Where are you from?" Shen Shen asks. "We've met others passing through from fifteen American states in the last three days."

"Us four from New York," Smiley says. "Him—" nodding at Muzzy— "from Tunisia, and him—" tipping head toward Seed— "from Iowa."

"When my brother arrived for summer term," Shen Shen says, "I told him about the *Unseeding America* Tour. He said he came here to learn, not to unlearn." She smiles, shakes her head. "Yesterday, we met another group and I told my parents about the tour."

Shen Shen walks us over to the church, pulls open the wooden door, leads us to where her parents, two of a group of five, all of them wearing light tan and grey suits, are seated in a pew. Shen Shen motions to her parents who rise and follow us outside.

Dad's about my height with short black hair, wife in long tan skirt, hair tied back tight in a ponytail.

"Y'all buying land for your government?" Moses asks.

"We own a private company," says Mom, accent mild.

"Our company make purchase of town, Chinese Camp," says Dad in a thicker accent. "And other towns in county."

"You ain't bought this church," Moses says.

"Yes, we do," Dad says. "Before us, diocese own church. Now we own."

"We understand there is no such thing as true ownership," Mom says.

"True enough to make some money," I say.

"Do you know the history of Chinese Camp?" Mom says.

"We know about the gold rush," Moses answers, "about that railroad y'all built."

"And the Tong wars?" she says.

We look at each other, shake our heads.

"When Chinese turn against each other," says Dad. "When we get some property, some business—laundry, gambling, brothel—and have to kill each other to protect it."

"Welcome to the U.S.A," Smiley says.

Mom inhales as if to speak, then pauses, and for a moment stands gazing out past the trees to the sinking light of the golden yellow valley.

"There was a woman in San Francisco named Madam Wan," she says, turning back. "Her body was cut into pieces by a Chinese gang from Oakland, each piece left at the door of one of her seven children. Madam Wan was my great great grandmother."

She looks from Moses to the rest of us, her eyes neither hard nor soft, just taking our measure.

"Now we make investment in land," says Dad.

"Y'all fixin to buy up the world," Smiley says.

"Someone will own it," mother says, "and someone will be trapped inside fighting."

"Might be a third option," I say, both parents looking at me, Shen Shen and little bro standing by. "Check it out." I open the *Unseeding America* app, show them the balance, north of 28 million dollars, flip through the ever darkening donation maps, most of Canada red, Mexico red, lightening to pink through Central and South America. I scroll across the Pacific: dark red from Japan spreading pink into China, Thailand, India.

"Having the cash," Moses says, "but not spending it."

"Letting potential energy stay potential," I say.

Shen Shen steps forward, takes her mother by both forearms and applies a slow firm kiss to her forehead. Then she does the same to her father.

We shake hands with the parents who walk back into the church, Shen Shen and little bro standing in place. Once the wooden door has swung closed behind them, Shen Shen tilts back her head, looks up at the sky, and spins in a circle.

We watch her complete several revolutions.

"The treetops are converging," she says, still spinning.

I tilt back and spin. "Yes," I say.

Moses, Connie, and Seed all lean their heads back, spin in a circle.

"Coming together like dancing angels," Shen Shen says.

"To dance on the head of a pin," I say, phrase coming to me from I don't know where.

Pausing, I check out little bro, watching us, turning back to the church, then back to me.

I smile and he smiles back, raises his eyes to the sky, and slowly spins. "Are they real?" he says.

"You see them, don't you?" Shen Shen says.

"Are they angels or trees?"

"Both," I say.

"Motherfuckers boogyin," Smiley says, head back, arms out to the side as he turns.

"Echebbi," Muzzy begins, pausing for Connie to comment, but Connie keeps spinning, gazing up at the converging treetops. "Echebbi says you can only imagine what already exists."

"So our parents should not buy the land," little bro says.

"Nah, man," Moses says, "your parents buyin up shit is cool."

"They doin what they need to," Connie says.

"We're the ones letting go," Seed says.

"The king of letting go," Moses says, throwing me a wink, offering a hand swipe as he turns.

Muzzy stops spinning and steps toward Shen Shen and her brother. "We understand your loyalty to your family," he says. "And to your country."

"Cause we all tribal," Moses says. "Just a question of what tribe pullin you in."

"Or pushin you out," I say.

Bus parked on the street starts its motor and opens its door, and we join the procession returning to board.

At the bus, little bro pulls Shen Shen aside, says something in Mandarin.

"Okay," Shen Shen says, and little bro pivots and runs back to the church, pulling the wooden door open with both arms, entering.

Shen Shen stands peering at the church, everyone else boarded except for Moses and me.

Finally, the wooden door pushes open and little bro comes running back to the bus.

"He asked our parents for next week's allowance to contribute to your account," Shen Shen says to Moses and me, little brother stopping before her "What did they say?" she asks him.

"They give it to me," he says. "Dad say they are going to miss us. Then Mom say, 'No, we miss what we leave behind. The children will be in front.'"

Shen Shen lays an arm across her brother's shoulders and ushers him onto the bus.

Couple minutes back on the road, sun dipping below the horizon, car headlights blinking on, Connie leans over and says to me, "So who their parents gonna leave that land to?"

I sit there peering out my window, the world shrinking away beneath the broad lavender sky.

"Theirs to keep," I say.

26

We arrive at midnight, the right lane clogged with parked busses, and have to walk a half mile or so just to reach the bridge, its two red towers illuminated like giant armor-clad sentries, the roadway bordered in lights, vertical lines rising up to meet great hanging suspension cables curving before a plum sky.

On the bridge, we find kids chillin in groups, sitting on the concrete barrier, playing hacky sack in the right lane, closed to traffic, some already up on the cables.

"Well, look what the cat drug in!" It's Hellcat, standing on the divider beside the walkway, head above a mob of girls busy in the closed lane, emptying backpacks, tossing gear—cables, pulleys, harnesses—onto growing piles.

"Y'all finally letting go!" I call to her.

"We ain't ever grabbed on!" she returns.

"Stolen land and borrowed time," I say.

We toss our loaded backpacks onto the piles, and Moses leads a pack of us back to the beginning of the suspension cable, climbs onto the concrete stanchion, up onto the steel-tubed suspension cable, the climb starting out mellow but getting steeper, and we grab onto the guide cables, one at shoulder height on each side, as we rise.

"That Verrazzano wasn't nothin!" Moses calls over his shoulder.

"Cause now we on the stairway to heaven!" I call back.

Up the Golden Gate we go, new arrivals below adding their gear to the piles, filing onto the cable behind us, ascending the far side, six lanes away, others climbing the vertical cables, till we pull ourselves onto the top of the first tower, take a seat, kids behind filing past, appearing from beneath, some hanging out on top, taking in the view, the night free of that famous harbor fog, others heading onto the downward cable toward the unoccupied center of the bridge.

"Yo, Staten Island!" Moses sings out. Sitting directly below, leaning out from the open arch of the tower, peering up at us, are Paisley and Long Shorts. "How the unforgivin doin today?" Moses calls.

"Good, man!" Paisley calls back.

"Still wearing that lucky flag?" Moses calls.

"Hell yeah!" Long Shorts answers.

"Check it out," Seed says, twisting around toward the other tower, half maybe three-quarters a mile away.

Barely visible, silhouetted before the halo of floodlight behind it, we see the nubby outline of the tower coated with kids, must be coming down from the north, suspension cables on both sides thick with bodies.

"We doin some Hitchcock shit now," Moses says. "Got us some *birds* on this motherfucker."

"They're still coming," Seed says, turned back to the San Francisco side where in the distance busses continue to pull over at the end of the line, switching on parking lights, each bus a glimmering gemstone added to the necklace curving through the darkness.

At the end of the line of busses, a black patch of hills, and beyond, the clustered light of San Francisco.

As I gaze out, noting the relationship of light to darkness, how bright the city is yet how dark, impervious the world around it remains, one spectral dot breaks free from the cluster, swings out over the water like some kind of slow-moving hologram.

Its blades beating the air, the chopper pauses first beside the far tower, then dips its nose and slides over to us.

"Congratulations, Little Man!" Bindermaus shouts through a megaphone out his open door. "You made it to the Pacific Coast!"

I stand up and take a bow in each direction, receive a weak smattering of applause.

"We've arranged transportation home for everyone!" Bindermaus says.

"He talkin bullshit," Smiley says. "We got thousands on this bridge and more comin."

"We're fine!" I shout to Bindermaus above the racket.

"You can't stay in California, Little Man! I don't care how much money you've raised!"

"Nobody stayin anywhere!" Moses calls.

Bindermaus turns toward the pilot, then back. "FBI needs you kids off the bridge!"

"Give us an hour!" I call.

"Okay, Little Man, one hour!"

The chopper spins away and shoots back toward the city.

Far as I can see both ways, every spot on the cables and in the tower arches is filled with bodies, the night again quiet, nothing but the soft whoosh of traffic far below.

I stand up, widen my base on the tower top, and shout as loudly as I can, "You motherfuckers ready?"

"First the phones!" Moses calls out, scrambling to his feet, turning on his phone flashlight, raising and waving it in the air, below us small lights blinking on, a growing sea of luminous dots rippling one way back to land, and the other way down the cables and up the far tower.

Phone at his shoulder, Moses executes a dramatic pivot and hurls it out into the night, its light rotating as it descends toward the harbor, and the next instant, thousands of tiny lights surge up into the darkness, blossoming like a huge firework and descending toward the water.

Except for mine, which I keep tucked in my pocket.

"Y'all motherfuckers bes start climbing to the top!" Moses calls out.

Moses steps over to me. "Look like we made it," he says.

"Yeah," I say.

Moses leans close, touches his scruffy cheek to my own. "Love you, bro," he says, takes two quick steps to the edge and is gone.

"I'm comin, dog!" Connie sings out, and he sidles past, swiping my hand, and jumps. Then Muzzy, then Seed—poof, just like that, gone—then Smiley, who pauses, looking back at me from the edge.

"Can't believe I'm here," he says, face glowing with gratitude.

"Where else you gonna be?" I say, and Smiley turns away and steps into the night, his body a brief falling shadow.

Shen Shen and her brother jump hand in hand, then Tommy and Hotah step to the edge, kids behind them crowding onto the surface, couple still with harnesses which they step out of, toss away.

I remove my phone. "Give me see some cheese-eatin' smiles," I tell Tommy and Hotah, and when they leap, they turn back into the camera flash, Tommy grinning with his tongue out, Hotah holding two thumbs up.

Next kid leaps and my flash catches him mid-pose, twisting back at the hips like he's aerial on a snowboard, one hand behind his head, the other reaching down for a board-grab.

Next two jump together, turning and facing each other as the flash goes off, shooting out fingers, odds or evens, next two playing Rock, Paper, Scissors.

The van driver from Pittsburgh steps up, nods at me, releases a sigh.

"Finally," he says, turns away, takes three steps, and is gone.

I snap pictures of another twenty or twenty-five jumpers, pause a moment to post them, instantly getting a response from a dude named Carleton Montgomery on the north tower, where he's posting his own pics, a selfie revealing the dude to be Abs, pics showing kids jumping in uniforms—football players, cheerleaders—others with face tats, eyebrow and lip rings, all the while, a steady stream of kids flowing past me on the south tower, out and off the edge.

"Some catcher in the rye you turned about to be!" It's Hellcat, moving along in line, Sheila and Tanika behind her.

"Time to *un*catch some motherfuckers," I say.

The three of them step to the side, letting others go past.

"Look like we gon see once and for all bout that dark energy," Hellcat says.

"Nothing to see about," I say.

"You that sure you gon be carried out to space?" she says.

"I know you're only a Spanish teacher," I say, "but damn, Hellcat, the point isn't what I do, what we do. If we go down, we're part of the 30 percent that goes down, that's all."

"Thirty-two percent," Sheila says.

"It ain't about us," I say.

Hellcat gazes at me, eyes shimmering in the light glancing off the towers. "You kids," she says with a smile. "One day, I'm out climbing a tree in Central Park, next day I'm flying off the Golden Gate Bridge, thinkin it don't matter which way I go."

"Cause it don't," Sheila says.

"Well, let's see," Hellcat says, stepping to the edge, kids beside her jumping one after the other.

She stops, looks back. "You kids," she says with a smile, turns back to the dark space and jumps, clasping one knee to her chest, rotating backward, dropping away into the night.

Kids keep filing past, jockeying for position, eager for their turn but also letting others go ahead, no reason to worry, knowing full well there's time and room for us all.

"Follow me," Sheila says, taking my hand.

"Just cause you're going first," I say, "doesn't mean I'm following."

"How bout I go first," she says, "but I follow you?"

Tanika nudges past us. "Talk talk talk," she says, blows us a kiss, and jumps.

I take my phone, pictures all posted, and toss it.

"Feels strange," Sheila says.

"Jumping off the Golden Gate Bridge?" I say.

"Like something around me is cracking, some kind of shell."

"I always knew you were a demon hatchling," I say.

"Fuck you," she says, stepping toward me, but I'm too quick to the edge, where I leap forward, Sheila leaping after me as I turn back in the rushing air to face her, unable to tell which way I'm moving, up, down, or both at the same time.

"Come get me, boy!" Sheila calls, her face a pale moon suspended in the darkness before me.

ABOUT THE AUTHOR

After growing up on the East End of Long Island in Amagansett, **Shelby Raebeck** spent time studying, playing a good deal of basketball (high school, college, and a lot of pick-up), teaching, coaching, and writing in such places as New York City, Boston, Florida, Louisiana, Utah, California, and Maryland, before returning to the East End to raise his two children, Talia and Sebastian.

Children now grown, he is currently at work on his next novel and, as always, seeking the next blue highway and hidden hiking trail.

ALSO BY SHELBY RAEBECK

LOUSE POINT: STORIES FROM THE EAST END

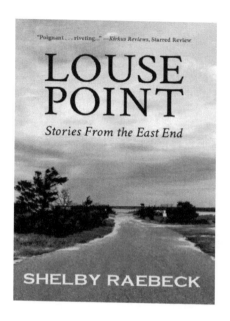

"Poignant…riveting…"
Starred Review, *Kirkus Reviews*

"Remarkable…ear-perfect…resonates with humanity."
Joan Baum, *Southampton Press*

"Sparkles with easy authority."
Beth Young, *East End Beacon*

SPARROW BEACH

"Intuitive, thoughtful, clever, shrewd."
Kirkus Reviews

"A warmhearted, thoughtful exploration of the inevitability of change,
even destructive change."
Catherine Langrehr, *IndieReader*

"A complex take on timely issues."
Joan Baum, *The Independent*

"A contemporary story that is both relevant and eye-
opening."
Reader's Favorite, Gold Medal Award